Indira Chandrasekhar is a scientist, a fiction writer and the founder and principal editor of the short fiction magazine, *Out of Print*. She has a PhD in biophysics and worked in scientific institutions in India, the US and Switzerland. She co-edited the short story anthology, *Pangea*, in 2012.

Praise for the book

Elegantly crafted, flawlessly paced, Indira Chandrasekhar's stories are still rivers whose depths are electric with unease. We are plunged, soon enough, into those depths. The social and cultural realities into which Chandrasekhar invites us seem reasonably familiar at first, but grow disorientingly strange. We look up from our reading, and everything that was previously normal pulsates with disturbance. Space, time, bodied identity, and family relationships: all are transmuted, fissured, shuffled in a labyrinth of unnerving futures. And often, as in the society founded on eugenics, divided between gated seafront citadels and illegal colonies, or the unequal exchange between a group of self-absorbed overseas anthropology students and the unwitting native informants whose family secrets they reduce cruelly to field work, or the psychologically troubled Bengali woman in a Nordic country who loses her children to the social services – we find ourselves uncomfortably back in the present. Indira Chandrasekhar's stories embody speculative fiction at its engaged, engaging best.

– Ranjit Hoskote

As is true of all the best short stories, there is never anything extraneous in Chandrasekhar's work, and furthermore, it is as if she sees everything and can *write* it... nothing is out of bounds to her; her reach is huge from the truly grisly to the utterly tender. Although Chandrasekhar's writing is superb literary work, it is also gritty, intimate and unabashed, and it is this precise combination which makes it so outstanding.

– Rebecca Lloyd

Intense and visceral, this is an elegant collection. Nothing in the sympathetic storytelling or the meticulous eye for detail prepares you for the hot, bleeding shock of brilliant endings. Strap your seatbelts on and trust Chandrasekhar to deftly take you on an unforgettable journey.

– Meena Kandasamy

POLYMORPHISM

STORIES

Indira Chandrasekhar

HarperCollins *Publishers* India

HarperCollins
PUBLISHERS
Since 1817

First published in India in 2017 by
HarperCollins *Publishers* India

Copyright © Indira Chandrasekhar 2017

P-ISBN: 978-93-5277-311-4
E-ISBN: 978-93-5277-312-1

2 4 6 8 10 9 7 5 3 1

Indira Chandrasekhar asserts the moral right
to be identified as the author of this work.

Cover art rendered from phase contrast microscope images of muscle cell
network in culture. Images taken by Abhijit Majumder, IIT Mumbai,
while a postdoctoral fellow under Jyotsna Dhawan, CCMB,
Hyderabad and inStem, Bengaluru.

Vector courtesy: Vecteezy.com

HarperCollins *Publishers*
A-75, Sector 57, Noida, Uttar Pradesh 201301, India
1 London Bridge Street, London, SE1 9GF, United Kingdom
2 Bloor Street East, Toronto, Ontario M4W 1A8, Canada
Lvl 13, 201 Elizabeth Street (PO Box A565, NSW, 1235),
Sydney NSW 2000, Australia
195 Broadway, New York, NY 10007, USA

Typeset in 11.5/16 Sabon LT Std
by Jojy Philip, New Delhi

Printed and bound at
Thomson Press (India) Ltd

To
Ila

CONTENTS

POLYMORPHISM

My shoulder was at it again, swivelling and turning like a mechanism lubricated with a heavy machine oil. I tried to pretend it wasn't happening, that my body wasn't giving in to the mobility, and I continued walking under the orange-red of the gulmohar trees. Just as I was losing myself in the brilliance of their elaborately bracted flowers, a man on a scooter veered towards me and snatched my bag, which yanked my arm right out of its socket. He must have been startled by how easily it dropped out, for I caught a split-second sight of his face – it seemed to widen grotesquely before he skidded and fell. But he was quick to recover. By the time I caught my breath, he had sped past the corner kiosk, leaving a crushed scarlet trail in the fallen flowers. My bag, with my medicines, was gone, and my arm was swinging about wildly.

I must start carrying my pills in my pocket, one part of my brain said, while another recalled techniques for getting out of panic mode – like counting to ten thousand three hundred and thirty-three, or breathing with my diaphragm. But such tricks, I was finding, are only useful well into the aftermath of an emergency, not during.

Like an injured homing pigeon, I fled erratically back towards the house. If I were fine, home would only have been seven minutes away, on a lane carpeted not red but lavender with jacaranda petals. I don't know how long it took me that day, but when I managed, finally, to crash through the front door and collapse, out of breath, on the cold tiles of the entrance hall, I could barely see from the headache and the pain. The lingering smell of the masala I had used in the brinjal fry that afternoon induced such a wave of nausea, it felt as if my head would burst, along with my gut.

'Ma,' Charu whispered in my ear, 'get up, get up. Mr Narasimhan is here for my maths tuition.'

'Aaaahhh,' I groaned, unable to rise.

'Shall I call a doctor?' I could hear Mr Narasimhan say. 'My sister's husband's cousin brother is a doctor and he lives in the next colony only. I can contact him.' His habitually rapid speech was more exaggerated than usual.

'No, no,' my daughter replied, 'it's nothing.'

'Nothing? But … but … oh, I see.' His tone turned sympathetic. 'Some ladies-type problems. His wife, that is my sister's husband's cousin brother's wife, is also a doctor, a ladies' specialist. Quite well known in her colony. She ...' Mr Narasimhan's voice rose in high-pitched excitement, causing my eardrums intense agony. My legs started to thrash around as I tried to get away from him.

'Manu, Manu!' my daughter bellowed. There was a complex series of sounds upstairs – chair pushed back, feet landing on the floor – each of which felt as if it were driving a hammer into my skull. As if to protect me, my auditory system seemed to sink into a fog as my son leapt down the stairs; everything sounded like it was travelling through some dense, absorbent substance and emerging muffled and warped. But his words were distinct enough. 'What? Couldn't you solve it? Don't worry. Here comes the calculus expert ...' He saw me and stopped abruptly. 'What the fuck!'

'The maths dude's here, Man,' Charu whispered. 'Watch your language.'

Manu bent over me. His mouth was open, his teeth – he really needed to see the dentist – seemed to move towards me ahead of his face. 'Come on, Ma,' he said, his voice gurgly as though he were under water. 'Let me take you to your room.' He lifted me up and staggered towards my bedroom that lay off the entrance hall. I could sense the warmth of his rangy young body as he held me, then settled me into bed. The pain began to dissipate and the sponginess in my ears began to clear somewhat.

'Mr Narasimhan,' I could hear Charu saying, 'this differentiation problem ... I need to answer it for tomorrow's class ...' She seemed to have succeeded in diverting him from my agonies; his voice rose in a happy squeak as he intoned the relevant rules of calculus. I could imagine my daughter's face glazing over; the sums would probably be the last thing she wanted to think about.

I wished Mr Narasimhan's voice had less ability to carry. He was slowing down, emphasizing, rounding out the words and pressing them into the rhythm of a mantra: 'Dee yex wover dee wai.' I didn't want to make fun of him, even in my head, but the combination of pain and muscle dysfunction made me unable to regulate myself. 'Dee yex ...' I mimicked, piercingly.

Manu gave me my pills and within minutes I felt relieved. My body was tightening and loosening in the right places, my shoulder was easing back, my tongue was under control. I was becoming human again.

He sat on the chair near my bed and watched me. The minute I could blink without my eyelids going into high-frequency mode, he said, 'How could you allow this to happen to you, Ma? Didn't you feel the symptoms? Your shoulder spinning? Faces melting? You didn't take your pill, did you?'

My voice was not quite back to normal and I deliberately made gagging sounds, hoping Manu's annoyance would turn to sympathy. But he just waited.

I thought of feigning incapacity – but one time when I had tried to get out of answering him about forgetting my medicines by pleading illness, I'd slipped up. My mind had wandered as I lay there, pretending to be too ill to respond to his queries; so when he'd leaned over with an anxious look, I felt the urge to make him smile and started telling him some long, gossipy story about the family. He was so angry that he grabbed me by the forearms, violently, as though he wanted to wrench my shoulder right out of its socket. I don't think he would actually have done it, but he most certainly would have screamed and cursed if he hadn't thought I was sick. In the end, he'd let go, ground his teeth, stood up and scolded me with great gravity. My poor little man. My condition had forced him into behaving like an adult.

Today, therefore, as soon as my system allowed, I explained to him about the man on the scooter who'd snatched my bag. He was horrified. I didn't want him to begin to worry every time I went out, so I said, 'My shoulder had started to give way by then, or I would have been able to snatch my purse back from the man. Or knock him off his bike.'

'You were that far gone? Before he attacked? You have to take the pill immediately, as soon as it shows itself. Why the fuck didn't you?'

'Don't swear,' I responded while I thought about what to say. How could I explain to him that I hadn't taken my pill because I wanted to savour my independence a little longer, wanted the freedom of walking without the oppressive thickening of the medication for just a few more steps?

But there was another reason why I wanted to delay my medication. One I couldn't share with anyone, least of all him. I could never admit to being tempted, every time, to give in, to relinquish control and allow my body to go where it would, where it could, and to take my mind with it. I had been close to the edge so often, had begun to sense the enticement of transformation so many times. But I had held back, terrified. For myself, for my children, my dear, sweet children ...

Now, however, it was almost irresistible drawing – me, pushing me to an extreme where every neuron was extended, maximally alive.

I lay back, silent, as Manu talked about managing my illness, and I felt sorry I had to impose so much on him. Each thread on my bedspread – a beautiful blue and pale-green printed cotton with a curiously European pattern of thistles and stalks, rather more widely spread than the fine Sanganeri flowers usually were – stood out, distinct and visible. The woody resinous aroma of eucalyptus mingled with the scent of jasmine and travelled in through the window, carrying colours with it – the waxy ivory and pink of frangipani and the ambers and ochres of the crotons. I was filled with a kind of hyper excitement, my chest quivering from having gone as far as I had, and I stretched up to hold the volatiles, elongating my extremities to immerse myself in them, allowing them to attach to me. Ecstasy. I could fly.

'Ma, Ma!' Manu's voice was loud. Loud and intrusive, taking me deeper into myself to try to escape it. 'Charu!' He was sobbing now, and I could feel him shaking.

'Please go, Mr Narasimhan.'

'You are not needing some help? I will stay, or bring the doctor.'

'Thank you, thank you, no, we don't need anything, please ...'

The front door banged and Charu, my beautiful Charu, came in on a cloud, no harsh sounds accompanying her. She lay her cool hand on my skin, which was brave of her, I know, because she had always been horrified, even as a little girl, when my skin began to mottle with the strange mobilities.

'Why, why?' Manu was saying. 'I was just here, watching her. Why did she let this happen; why didn't she ask me for another pill?'

I drifted back towards my other existences where everything was intensely felt, every sensation magnified. I was a stretched, vibrating string, highly tuned, separated from the low noise of everyday. I could do anything; I was alight.

But Manu was loud, holding my arms, shouting

at me, interfering. I began to hear the words he was saying and participate in the children's emotions even as I strove to float above and shape my world in wild and wonderful ways. 'The thing is, Man,' I heard my daughter say gently, 'I know why Ma's done it. It's happened to me too. Feels like magic.'

Manu's breath turned to desperate, gasping sobs, full of loss and fear. Just as it did when his various cats died, and his father ... Whenever it happened, he would collapse into me, clutching my shoulders, leaning into me. And even after I was weakened by the increasing frequency of the morphing, I always found the strength to bear his weight till he could breathe again.

'Pull yourself together, Man. I am here. I won't go away. I can come back from the other state whenever I want.'

'I can come back too,' I called out. 'I can do anything, I can come back too.'

'Watch out, she's starting to vibrate, stay out of her way.'

'She won't hurt us, Manu. She knows us.'

But Manu wasn't listening. He was backing into the wall and screaming, 'Get out, lock the door.'

'It's her, Man, it's Ma. Just stay quiet and nothing will happen.'

'Yes, yes, listen to Charu, it's me,' I responded, but as my external vocal chords began to resonate, the words disappeared into the giant buzzing sound they made.

I had to stop or I would slice my children into bits. I tried to hold my abdomen tight so as to control it all, but I couldn't any more. I was panicking. The sound reached a higher and higher pitch.

'Manu, Manu!' I could hear my daughter. But I couldn't see anything any more as I started to rise and hit the walls and the ceiling. I could hear glass break, and the fragrance of the perfume my daughter had given me pervaded the air and entered the pores of my underbelly, oversweet and strong. I bent down to look.

'Now!' I heard them shout. I felt Charu's cool hand on my tight, tense body, reaching to still the viciously sharp chord. I could feel Manu's firm, warm grasp. I had to stop from moving or their fine young skin would be cut, their flesh lacerated. I tried to breathe and count to three thousand six hundred and seventy-three, even as I tasted their blood.

INTENSIVE CARE

I concentrated on breathing at the same pace as Sarasa: shallow in, shallow out. My eyes were almost shut, dimming the murky green light that filtered through the curtain drawn across the glass panel of the intensive care ward.

Two nurses stepped into the cubicle, talking loudly. 'Shh, patient's relative is here, sleeping,' one of them whispered.

'No problem,' the other replied. 'It's only her daughter. Comes daily and sits.'

I raised my eyelids. I could see her faint outline. As she approached the bed, she switched on the wall lamp, which threw her face and then the starched front of her uniform into harsh, blue-white relief. The other nurse, the younger one, moved in and out of the sharp shadow as she bent over the chart and then checked Sarasa's drip.

'Oh god, next patient is that old man,' the young nurse said with a titter.

I didn't hear the other nurse respond. But when I opened my eyes and glanced over, I saw her lips extend ever so slightly and her almond eyes elongate, drawing out the grey shadows under her lower lids. She seemed strangely excited.

The young nurse continued, 'Stupid man. Always crying "pain, pain". As if everyone in this ward doesn't have pain.'

The older woman smiled, and I felt afraid.

They went into the next cubicle. 'Aah, aah,' I heard a man crying.

The two nurses made faint bird-like sounds. I couldn't tell whether they were laughing or making kind, soothing, clucking noises. But then the younger one exclaimed, her voice pitched high, 'Are you moving the needle inside his vein? You are, aren't you?'

The other nurse laughed, then said in a low, sibilant hiss, 'See, old man, you shouldn't have complained about me to my supervisor.'

It was after that episode that Sarasa had begged to be allowed to come home. But the more she begged, the more determined Rajiv was that she should stay in the hospital and try the new treatment. 'They say even your hair will grow back. You have to try,' he pleaded.

∽

Sarasa is finally home now and her hair *is* long, but if you touch her, even lightly, she screams in agony.

'My follicles have ripened,' she explains in a whisper when the pain has settled. Occasionally she exclaims dramatically, 'My skin, my flesh, aflame.'

It reminds me that she used to write poetry. On one of my birthdays, the tenth or the eleventh, I told her she could send the poem she'd written for me to a magazine if she wanted to, but she laughed and hugged me and said, 'They think it's dreadful sentimental stuff. These are only for you and me, sweetie.' I was happy and hugged her back.

If you press your fingers on her body, they make a sanguine impression on her fair skin. 'It's her blood vessels,' Rajiv explains. 'They are so fragile that they fracture and bleed under the pressure.' He demonstrates and she cries. 'Only for a second, Saras – don't cry, darling,' he says. But he is not concerned about her pain; only proud that he can show her off again.

In the earliest image of Sarasa I carry in my mind, she is in front of the wall mirror, combing her long hair. The electricity has failed. As she lifts her comb at the end of each stroke, the hair lifts too, and a shower of sparks crackles. I thought she had turned into a goddess and would rise into the sky and leave me, and I began to cry.

Rajiv, who'd been sitting in an armchair, watching Sarasa, roared with laughter at my tears. 'What do you think? That your mother is on fire?' he asked, making whooshing fire sounds. Sarasa had picked me up then and cradled my head on her shoulder, and said, 'She's so little, darling, don't tease her.'

It would be another two years before Rajiv moved in permanently with us. Almost as if apologizing to me for her happiness, Sarasa had said, 'Now we won't be alone.' But we were never alone, we had each other, I wanted to say. I want to ask her about it now but I know she doesn't have the strength.

Sarasa smells different these days. Her blood lives close under her skin; so she smells of iron and salt. And a kind of rot, as if the plasma seeps through the membranes and putrefies in the air. Every now and then, a red drop extrudes from a random spot on her body and drips, like an unacknowledged, unnoticed tear of blood. I watch as one slides down her forearm. If it stains the white sofa, she will notice and be upset.

I hold her ever so softly and walk her, two steps, to the window. She leans on me.

'Kiki,' she calls. The neurotic black cat that Sarasa rescued from the streets looks up at the sound of her name. Kiki understands how fragile Sarasa is; maybe it's because of the smell, but there are no more rough, abandoned, rolling, scratching sessions. She is delicate in her encounters with Sarasa.

Far more so than Rajiv, who badgers Sarasa, insisting she get dressed every morning, brushing her hair even when she cries out that it hurts.

I have brought out my baby brush that was stored,

along with other memorabilia, at the back of my drawer. It was meant for a newborn. But I received it when I was a toddler. It was already too soft for my hair, so it is practically unused, its bristles soft and new. It was a present from Sarasa's sister. 'I didn't realize you'd taken in a toddler, Sarasa. You told me she was a baby. But she must be two at least,' she had said, gesturing towards the minuscule clothes she'd unpacked from her suitcase. 'She is. Just a baby,' Sarasa replied quietly, hugging me tight. 'Well,' my aunt said, shrugging, 'pass the clothes to Rajiv's sister. Her little one is a few months old; not a few years.' She'd handed me the brush as the other pretty things disappeared into a shiny bag.

I want to ask Sarasa where I come from, where she found me. We found Kiki at the seafront. 'She was two-dimensional when we found her, two-dimensional from starvation,' Sarasa used to say. 'But look at her now!' We would watch as Kiki, her stomach plump, her hair a glistening black, tried to grab a trickle of water running out of the tap. 'She's not afraid of the water, our Kiki of the sea.'

The first kitten we ever rescued, years before Kiki arrived, was a ginger fellow with a demanding voice. We'd found him, small and hungry and loud, by a construction site. The early years of starvation seemed to make him permanently desperate for food. It used to drive Rajiv crazy. 'I'm going to smother this creature – no peace in the morning! I can't leave my toast untended for a minute,' he had yelled when the kitten helped himself to some of Rajiv's food once again. This time he looked as if he was really going to hurt the kitten, so I grabbed him and hid him under my teddy-bear quilt. Sarasa extricated him, saying, 'You'll cut off his air supply, sweetie. You can't bury him under the quilt like that.'

As I continued to cry, she said, 'Don't worry, Rajiv will learn. Shall we explain that the kitty can't help it, that he was just so hungry when he started life that he's trying to get full now? You and I know it takes a long time to forget what we learn when we are little, don't we, love?'

We had to put the ginger kitten down when he got hit by a car. Sarasa and I sat by him, watching till his breath died down and he was gone.

'She is deteriorating. I am going to arrange for professional care,' Rajiv is saying on the phone. 'Yes, those girls from the hospital will come in after duty, start this week.' Then he says, 'Yes, I remember that nonsense about those nurses hurting her. It was all in her mind ... or "sweetie's". The nurses are perfectly competent.'

I am breathing with Sarasa again: shallow in, shallow out. I can barely move, I am taking in so little air. When I was young I would lie on top of her and we would breathe – in together, out together. 'This way our lives are connected,' she would say. We would breathe together till the air between us got too warm and moist, or one of us started laughing. I cannot lie on her now. I cannot even touch her any more. But I can watch her chest rise and fall, and I can breathe with her.

'What have you done, you stupid, wild creature! What have you done,' Rajiv is yelling. He throws off sari upon sari, roughly tossing aside even the delicate silk ones I had spread so carefully on her without a single crease.

Sarasa would have been proud I had taken so much care. The innermost layer was her mother's cotton sari, soft and light from a million washes. It didn't press down on Sarasa's poor inflamed skin. And neither did any of the next layers. I had made sure there was no pressure on her, just the gentle weight of a cupboardful of her favourite saris moving ever more feebly with her breath.

When I couldn't breathe with her any longer, I simply sat and watched till all movement stopped.

ADORATION

I fell in love with her when I was nine. It was her skin –
such a beautiful golden-cream colour, like condensed
milk, but luminous. I felt that if I could lick it, secretly,
without leaving a slimy trace of my saliva to sully
its perfection, I would taste heaven. And I can't even
describe the heights of heaven I reached a few years
later when I imagined myself tasting other more secret
surfaces.

All just foolishness – I will never get close enough
to smell the great Devipriya, let alone taste her.

I did see her once, at a function at the trade fair
grounds. The tall chain-link fences that surrounded
the premises dripped with people and those who'd
climbed the highest were triumphant. But all they
could see, the idiots, was the top of her head – her
hair was a bright orange-pink for the movie she was
shooting then.

I knew how to get a better view; I arrived early,

tied a scented kerchief around my nose and clambered halfway – not all the way – up the fence to a spot directly over the canal that bordered the slum on the other side of the grounds. It was the best position, a perfect angle for viewing. When she glanced up, I caught sight of her face framed by the links, and I thought I would die. But I willed my melting limbs to hang on because I didn't want the moment to end in the stinking canal.

The funny thing is, although seeing her like that was brilliant, I mean truly brilliant, it was also frustrating. She was gone in five minutes and I didn't get enough time to sink into the vision.

My neighbour has a DVD player. When he's away, I climb into his flat and use it. If I am sharp, I can pause the disc just when her smile is directed straight at me. They say that the eyes define a person – windows to the soul and all. She has eyes to write poetry about. But it's her lips, that delicate bow dimpling into the soft roundness of her cheek, it's her lips that reveal her inner beauty. It's not only the shape, it's that fine ridge around them, luscious and pure, which opens up the contours just a little bit more.

The film *Basanti* is one of the few where it's not her face I want to dissolve into. When she lifts her arm to toss the colours of Holi at the hero, I see a slight crease in her golden skin where the material of her sleeve pulls at it. And if I manage to halt the film at the

right frame, I can see a hint of the luscious weight that
drags at her blouse. Need I say more?

∽

Salim and I met as kids in the queue for tickets to
Basanti. He lived in a joint family, so no one noticed
if he was around or not. He'd sneak off to follow our
idol wherever she appeared. In those days you could
get close when they were shooting on the streets. Not
like now, where the outdoor scenes are shot in foreign
countries and the studios where the indoor scenes are
filmed are impossible for anyone to get into … except
for Salim, the lucky fucker, who seems to have made it
into the inner circle and goes wherever she goes.

I bumped into him at Orion Mall. She was expected
at the first anniversary celebration. Salim was in the
inner enclosure, part of her entourage, the slimy shit.

I fought my way to the front and called out, 'Wow,
Salim bastard! You look great. Muscles like the big
stars, man.'

His shoulders bulged under his tight tee shirt. Even
his crotch seemed to have doubled in size, his thighs
looking scrawny in comparison. He laughed, let me
past the security, slapped me on my back and said,
'Bastard! Mummy let you out today? Just teasing,
man, don't look so pissed.'

He turned to the others. 'This bastard is a major
fan. No movie he hasn't seen of our Devipriya-ji. His

room …' I had made the mistake of taking him home once. My mother freaked at having a Muslim kid, practically from the slums, in our house. She counted her glass artefacts after he left.

'You've got to see his room, man – papered with posters. Her breasts leaning over his bed. At night …' he added, with a meaningful shake of his head.

The others laughed. I laughed too, feeling sick.

She didn't show up at the Orion Mall anniversary event. Held up at shooting, they announced. Her troupe exchanged significant looks as they packed up.

'Shit, don't look so sad, man. Come with me. I'll take you to her.'

I didn't believe Salim but I went along.

The apartment building was on a corner of a quiet street, the entrance narrow and grotty. I peered through the accordion grill doors as the lift rose slowly past two empty floors. The light from the lift lit up the rubble that crumbled off the disintegrating walls. Water dripped somewhere and a damp smell pervaded the air. 'The building used to belong to her mother, man, Supriya Devi. Remember her? She lived on these floors – totally abandoned since she died.'

Supriya Devi! She too had been a famous movie star. Stopped acting at the peak of her career. There was some scandal – the teenage daughter had an affair with the mother's lover, wasn't that it? No, it couldn't be, her only child was our beautiful Devipriya. The scandal erupted thirty years ago. My Devipriya could not have been a teenager then; she must have been a little girl – too pure, too young to have an affair.

'Don't make a noise, man, in case she's resting,' Salim whispered as we entered the apartment. It was very dark but I could see marble gleaming and reflecting off opulent mirrors. We climbed a carpeted stairway.

'This is my room,' Salim said, and turned on the light. It looked fancy but I didn't pay much attention, for, at that moment, Salim reached into his trousers and groped, making little whimpering sounds. 'Wow, fuck man, it's so hot,' he said, and yanked. As I backed quickly towards the door, something landed at my feet. It was a padded, cup-shaped object, a sponge in a stocking, Barbie-doll-flesh coloured, pungent with sweat. Before I could move, he removed his tee shirt. Underneath was another layer, skin-tight, that he stripped off. It flopped, grey-white, beside him. Before me stood the old, puny Salim.

He laughed at my expression and said, 'No one but Hrithik has real muscles, man. But those fucking ready-made padded suits are fucking expensive. My sister makes mine for me. Cool, no?' He held up his sweaty vest and palpated the sponge at the shoulder before tossing the vile thing on the back of a chair. 'Free, man, shit, I don't pay a paisa for the padding, they're *her* used cups.' He carved spheres in space in front of his chest. 'Poor thing, our beauty has nothing, man. Almost flat, has to wear cups even in summer, shooting in the heat. Bad rashes.'

'Come.' He led me out. 'You want to see her dressing room?' It was a long room finished in white veneer with ornate gold trim detaching in places. A cupboard door hung off its hinges. On a shelf against a mirrored wall were stands holding wigs – black, brown, orange-pink. 'Look, that's from the New York movie, you recognize?' To think it wasn't her own hair!

I was appalled at how Salim fingered her things with his unwashed hands. 'Careful, man,' I said as he picked at a bead on one of her bodices.

He laughed and replied, 'Take it easy, bastard. She won't be using it soon – too thin to fill her bodysuits.' He pulled out a garment. It was body-shaped, a thick polymer material, golden-cream – a full body stocking. I couldn't hide my horror.

'What? You didn't think her skin colour was real?' He cackled manically and led the way into the corridor. A large red-brown cockroach scuttled along the edge, keeping pace with us. Salim opened the door of a bedroom and the roach darted in, its antennae waving. A nightlight glowed on a bedside table on which sat dinner, barely touched.

The room was chilled and stale smelling. A figure lay huddled under a quilt. Salim turned on a lamp with a dimmer switch. As the room brightened, I saw that the figure was a woman with a ravaged, dark face. Her hair, sparse and wispy on the unwashed pillow, was a coarse black, but a band of greasy grey lined her face. An arm lay outstretched on the quilt, the saggy skin an unhealthy brown.

The woman coughed and stirred. 'Salim? What took you so long? Have you got it?'

Salim stepped forward. 'Shh,' he said. He picked up a hypodermic from a steel plate on the dresser and took out a glass vial from his pocket that he held up to the light.

She grabbed his hand. 'Hurry, Salim, hurry,' she quavered. 'You kept me waiting so long, don't taunt me now.'

He tapped the vial with a rusty blade. The cockroach, now sitting on the yellow dal, raised its head and waggled its antennae inquiringly.

Revolted, I started to leave the room. Devipriya lifted her head. She looked straight at me and smiled. The fine ridge around her lips picked up the light, opening up the contours that little bit more, and she seemed to glow, a luminous golden-cream. I smiled back, in heaven.

BLACK SARI

Five of us shared the makeshift dormitory in the front hall of the old house. Our landlady, a young widow, lived in separate quarters across the central courtyard. She maintained a strict and pure regimen, and her clothes, her food, even the air she breathed, didn't mingle with our multiple other castes. Every week, we placed our rent money in a bronze tray that she put across the threshold between her quarters and ours. I would look up from the tray and see her watching me. She would smile, say thank you in a soft voice, and ask me how I was.

We called her Akka – older sister. It seemed a more appropriate term than Amma because she certainly wasn't old enough to be our mother. Apart from that, Amma seemed a cruel term for a childless widow who mourned the children she would never have.

One day, Akka decided to start feeding us. 'I am cooking anyway,' she said. 'Come taste my food.'

We rolled up our sleeping mats, lined them against the wall and cleared space on the floor to lay out the banana leaves she'd purchased for the purpose. Akka bent over the threshold to pour the sour, vibrant, stew-like hulli she had prepared, into vessels that were going to be banished from the kitchen once we had used them. She made sure to hold the cooking vessels at least six inches above the soon-to-be-banished serving ones placed on the floor. She then ate by herself on the other side of the door – pollution free, unsullied. Occasionally she'd call out a question to which we would shout the answer, but mostly, she was silent. In the hall, we gossiped as one of us ladled the food out on to the leaves. When we finished, we put what was left into a clay pot for the beggar lady who came every night, rinsed the banished pots and put them back by the threshold for the next day. And one of our group, Siddi, volunteered to wipe the floors; she was from a lower caste. I think we all felt that order was maintained.

After some time, the many filters against caste pollution began to get Akka down. 'I am always washing away some impurity, cleansing something,' she complained for over a month as she hung out her wet sari, or shivered in it while she chanted near the tulsi plant in the courtyard. One day, she gave us steel plates in place of the banana leaves. 'I sold a gold chain that some relative had given at my wedding and bought these,' she said. 'If my in-laws come, you have to say they are yours. Although I am sure they won't ever come here. They want me to hold a purification ceremony – a fire-cleansing in the hall – before they will step in.'

One afternoon, Akka called me and beckoned to me to step across the threshold. It was a Tuesday, my day off – early enough that the two schoolteachers with their relentless chatter weren't back yet and no one else was in the house. 'Can you help me?' she asked. We walked towards the dark inner chambers on the other side of the courtyard. It was an area I had never even glimpsed before. Her body, as she walked in front of me, seemed to vibrate. As I crossed the stone paving, I wondered what had happened. Had she become pregnant somehow? She was young and I, who now spent almost an hour a week with the creepy son of my employer, knew what it was like to yearn for someone's, anyone's touch. We entered her bedroom in the middle of which sat an old rosewood bed covered with a thin, ill-fitting cotton mattress. She lay down on it, lifted her sari up, opened her legs and repeated, 'Can you help me?'

It became a little routine, a private, secret routine we never spoke about. One day I kissed her on the lips – until then our salivas had never mingled – and she smiled. Not long after, Akka began to ask us to enter the kitchen to help with the cooking and the serving.

∽

Shantamma disapproved of Akka's newfound laxity in the kitchen and would frown whenever any of us, especially Siddi, stepped across the threshold into the now-sullied cooking area. Sometimes Shantamma would begin to scold, her voice wearing us all down until we retreated to the hall, Akka to her room, and pretend to go to bed.

Shantamma belonged to a northern Karnataka group that had broken away from caste centuries ago. She was proud of this, and proud of belonging to a subgroup that had converted from a higher caste into this ideal of equality. We never marry outside our subgroup, she would declare.

The village that she came from had been in drought for many decades. When she described it, we imagined ground that was dry and concave and impacted and cracked. As if something in the earth's core was sucking away all the residual moisture. She told us that when they peed in the field next to their huts, the liquid would, at first, float on the scabbed surface because there were no pores left in the soil to draw the water in, but when it reached the cracks it disappeared so fast that they imagined a beast with manic, sucking tongues sat beneath, waiting to consume the liquid. 'We were afraid to straddle the cracks for fear his tongues would reach into us and suck us dry,' she said. 'This fear held the girls so taut that they stopped menstruating. But,' she added, 'before that happened to me, I gave birth, three, maybe four, maybe five times, all dry and dead before they were even born.'

Starvation, and hard lifting in her job as a nurse attendant had made Shantamma narrow and tight waisted. But the daily rice-based meal at Akka's caused her to expand until a firm round bowl seemed to be suspended at her middle. She was given to letting forth loud burps, painful-sounding passages of intestinal gas that made their way up her abdominal tract and burst out of her mouth in little shrieks. Whenever this happened, her neat round face would contort and her lips would part, revealing worn-down, blackened stubs. She was very conscious of her damaged teeth and usually kept her lips firmly closed. If you made her laugh, and her teeth showed in the abandonment of the moment, her mirth would instantly change to resentment and anger and she would accuse you of mocking her. I learnt never to tell stories in her presence but only to listen to hers so she did not have to be surprised into opening her mouth and revealing her stubs. I thought it made her like me a little.

∽

One day Shantamma surprised us by taking out a bunch of saris from her metal storage trunk. We fingered the luscious materials with envy.

'The lady gave them to me,' she said.

'Which lady, the old lady you take care of?' we asked.

Shantamma frowned. 'No, no, I've told you. Rani Bai can't move, can't speak. She lies in a white medical bed all day. Every two hours I must turn her. I lift her body and shift it to a new position and she just rolls into place like a dry, shrunken bundle. She can't give me saris! But she knows they are there, all right. The old woman has forgotten all her relatives but she does remember she has *things*. Thinks everyone is taking them away from her. When she points to one of the cupboards, I have to wheel her there to open it and check what is inside. Yes! And if it's locked, as many are, I have to show her I am checking the locks with a tug. If I don't do it immediately, as soon as she points, she starts shaking and screaming.'

'So who gave you the saris, then?'

'Don't you follow anything? The young lady, Mini gave them!' she exclaimed. Nobody dared point out that she had not told us about Mini. 'She is Rani Bai's granddaughter's daughter. Comes to visit every three or four months. She has the keys to everything, and when she arrives she shakes them in front of the old woman and speaks very loudly. "Hi Ajji."' Shantamma contorted her cheeks and imitated the granddaughter's English: 'Clean cupboard clean.'

We laughed.

Shantamma was pleased and continued, 'How the old woman hates it when Mini is there. Shakes her head, making gargling noises.' Shantamma demonstrated. 'Last time, Mini threw away piles and piles of papers. "Bond, useless, bond," she said. The old woman clutched her head with her hands and banged it up and down.' Shantamma laughed.

I myself had only recently cleared out bonds from my parents' safe when they died, discovering they were obsolete and that I was penniless.

'When Mini took the saris out of the cupboard, the old woman began to wail. "Don't cry, Ajji, they are useless," Mini said as she tossed them into the corner of the room, a big black pile. The old woman shrieked and shrieked. Later, when she was locking up, the girl pointed to the saris in the corner. "Take them," she said to me. "Nobody here is going to wear them." To appease the old woman, I folded them up after Mini left and tucked one or two under the mattress. "That way, she can't take them away the next time she comes," I told her. The old lady held my hand and gave me a gold coin from the bag under her pillow. Didn't she know I had already taken most of them? Luckily she picked a good coin rather than one of the five-rupee brass ones I had put in as substitutes.'

'You took the coins?'

'Yes, what is that stinking old lady going to do with them anyway? I deserve something for cleaning her shit every day. Better to take them than to let the stupid night nurse get them.'

'What did you do with the coins?'

'Those things?' Shantamma smiled slyly and did not respond. But she did reach into her blouse and show us a beautiful coin, with a double-headed eagle, the old palace insignia, on one side.

The saris had a strange attraction. I could feel their weight on me, their voluptuousness when I draped them on myself. They were, without exception, woven in solid dark colours – blacks, browns and maroons, colours that were devoid of brightness. No lines of orange, no blue checks, no temple borders with yellow outlines to alleviate the density. Despite the darkness of the weave and the quality the fabrics had of drawing the light into them, they were rich and radiant.

When I was particularly unctuous, Shantamma would allow me to wear one of the saris. It sat with a sort of old-fashioned grace on me that I loved.

One day, Shantamma gave me one of the saris, a black one, and some of the dark brown ones to Akka. 'Take them,' she said, with a sly smile that I wondered about. But I was so thrilled to have the silk that I did not worry too much about whether her intention might be malicious. As for Akka, I could tell that the thought of wearing a sari which had sat against unknown skin took a great deal of inner resolve to overcome; so she was not paying attention to Shantamma's expression.

'You know what the saris are?' Shantamma asked a month or two later, forgetting to purse her lips and grinning widely. We all stared at her. Akka, who now spent the evenings participating in our daily routines, was combing my hair. She stopped, mid-stroke, and I stayed frozen even though a single hair was caught in the teeth of the comb and pulling at my scalp. 'To catch the blood,' Shantamma said, triumphantly. Once she'd said it, it seemed obvious. They were menstruation drip saris, menopause-overflow saris, fibroid-bleed saris, saris that masked the excess that the body and the blood-catching cloths wedged between the legs could not hold, saris that were reminders of our empty wombs.

We all stirred. All of our blood flows had increased in the last months, especially Akka's and mine. We had convinced ourselves that our bodies were influenced by each other, sympathetic responses, but now it crossed all our minds that it was the saris that were wringing the fluids from us. Akka stopped wearing them, even though they had made her happy and glow like a goddess – she still hoped for children although nobody, not even she, knew who was going to impregnate her. I, on the other hand, revelled in the freedom from worrying about becoming pregnant, the freedom the saris seemed to be giving me by making my womb bleed.

∽

Akka stopped asking me into her room.

Shantamma smirked and pursed her lips the first time Sunanda – or was it Lakshmi? – replaced me. I had assumed I had been very discreet. But I suppose everyone knew.

Initially, I missed it, and missed her, and was jealous of the newer, younger residents she smiled at. Then I realized that what I missed most was the quiet hour away from everyone in Akka's cool dark room.

ANY DAY NOW

Mrs M's flat used to be sparse and shabby when Vira roomed there during her college years. The furniture was upholstered with a flimsy off-white material that had turned brown in patches, and there were no pictures, no photographs, and little evidence of Mr M who had moved in with another woman. 'I left her the flat, goddamn it,' he was known to have said to mutual friends. Mrs M told Vira that when he left, she threw out the ornate ceiling fans and satin bedspreads, stripped the sofa by ripping off its shiny flowery material so only the lining remained, got rid of the glossy black-topped bar with its metal beading and glass cabinets, and had begun to take in students as paying guests.

Most of the time, Vira was the only boarder. Because even though the beds were comfortable, the rooms filled with light, and the food adequate if uninspired, most of the other law students from the nearby college were unable to handle the grim loneliness that surrounded Mrs M. But the atmosphere of grief sloughing off into a deeply embedded solitariness was just what Vira needed. She was trying to make a life for herself outside the circle of weeping, caring relatives who didn't seem to understand that she couldn't function when she was constantly reminded of the plane that had crashed between Bangalore and Delhi and ended her parents' lives in what she assumed was a screaming, fearful, searing conflagration that blackened their faces and twisted their bodies beyond recognition.

Her room in the flat was a retreat where she kept the curtains drawn, and into which she admitted no one and where nothing bright intruded. When she wasn't in bed, she would read her notebooks filled with the day's lectures, drawing faces in the margins. This allowed her to focus on her parents' smiles as they'd said goodbye and remember the many times they had exclaimed how proud they were that they had created someone as special as her. It was the only way she was able to do everyday things, such as brush her hair and go to class.

In their respective silences, Mrs M and Vira developed a friendship that had sustained them, and her landlady became an odd, ill-equipped surrogate parent to Vira. That's why, whenever things got shaky, she yearned for the quiet of Mrs M's flat.

∽

It was a shock, therefore, to discover that Mrs M had stopped taking in boarders and had, instead, acquired friends and visitors in the three years Vira had been away. The sofa was now a sleek orange piece of furniture with a bold paisley print, and sported a collection of dark velvet cushions. Photographs of paying guests, who had apparently ended up staying longer than a few weeks, leaned against piles of magazines on the previously bare table. Vira remembered the old nails on the greying corridor wall, ghostly reminders of the florid Mr M, that had stuck out unadorned and framed by shadows. Now, there were calendars with pictures of gods hanging there that Mrs M said had been given to her by 'the servants'; 'I can't throw them away, can I? They'd be offended.' To Vira, the most bizarre of all the changes was the servants, a fluid collection of people who were apparently there to assist Mrs M in running the house. They floated through the flat and did not seem to do much, and Mrs M certainly seemed to have no ability to direct them.

Simi, whose job included helping to lay the table, came mincing into the dining room swaying her narrow hips, a parody of the coy television heroines who always retained their virtue even as they seduced hosts of men and begat children out of wedlock during amnesiac spells. As soon as Simi entered, Mrs M scolded her for flirting with the driver. 'Don't lead him on like that. Anything can happen!'

'Nothing will happen, Amma. I am true to my Mohan, don't you know,' the girl responded.

Vira frowned as Mrs M returned to the kitchen without answering. The girl needed to be pulled up, stopped from flirting with the men. 'Maybe *you* are true to him, but *they* can't be trusted, those fellows ...' Vira began, but stopped when she saw the girl's face. It was as if Simi couldn't hear anything being said. Instead, moving closer to the table, she giggled. 'Mohan and I, we will be married in October. We are fixing a date soon. Will you be here? You must come, you must.'

Vira returned to her laptop screen. Yesterday she had cut up the sari she was to have worn for her own wedding. 'What a silly waste,' Mrs M proclaimed in a shaky voice as Vira sat surrounded by shreds of papery, honey-gold, silk tissue. 'I would never allow a daughter of mine to do this.' When Vira didn't respond, Mrs M continued, 'You could have sold the sari, or given it to the girl to use at her wedding.' What? This piece of fabric that has only brought me bad luck? Vira wanted to scream. But she didn't, and Mrs M started to sweep the bits together, saying, 'Clear it up before the girl gets back from visiting her fiancé's family. We can't have her see this.'

Vira had placed the clear polythene bag of destroyed idiotic hope in the middle of her suitcase and shut and locked it.

Simi turned on the overhead lamp and an ephemeron lifted towards it, then fluttered down to the mosaic tiles, losing its exquisite wings. Vira watched as it turned from flying gauze to dumpy earth-bound mortality. Her contemplation of its clumsy writhing body was interrupted as the girl thrust a glittering necklace of red and gold plastic beads at her. 'Look at these, Akka. Look.'

'Shut the windows. The insects have emerged; they'll head for the light,' Mrs M called from the kitchen.

Already, more ephemera hovered around the bulb, falling quickly to the floor, leaving behind papery, translucent piles of wings as the ants hurried to consume their defenceless bodies. The successful ones have probably already deposited the next generation in some secret dark place, Vira thought. She was almost certain she was one of the successful ones of her species. But the joy that had first lifted her when she had suspected she was expecting a child and believed that, like her parents, she too would create something wonderful, lay discarded, and the idea of a new generation left her feeling drained and uncertain.

'Look, Akka, look. You are not looking.' Simi's hand was directly in front of Vira, clutching a bunch of gleaming bright pendants and eardrops made from gilt-coated polymer and cheap alloy.

The girl's face shone with a strange eagerness, and Vira found it impossible to ignore her. 'Very pretty,

Simi,' she said, picking up a pendant and holding it high.

She was startled by the girl's shriek. 'Aieeo, my name's not Simi any more! Didn't she tell you?' The girl was pointing at Mrs M, who entered the room carrying hot rice in the white ceramic bowl with its border of blue flowers. Vira remembered that the bowl used to be taken out on special occasions and smiled, wondering if it was being used in her honour. Mrs M smiled back, as if acknowledging that it was. But before she could say anything, Simi repeated, 'My name's not Simi any more,' in a high-pitched voice accompanied by a wild, whickering laugh.

Mrs M turned. 'Come, come, child. Didn't you hear me calling from the kitchen? Go bring the dal.'

The girl stared for a moment. Then she picked up her things and slipped them back in the transparent ziplock bag, stepping back and forth all the time as if to a tune in her head. 'Not Simi any more,' she said. 'They've changed my name to Mohanapriya. Priya means beloved, don't you know? Mohan's beloved.' The smile left her face and she added, 'The astrologer says that the old name doesn't set with my Mohan's. Maybe that's why the wedding has been delayed again.'

Vira was paralysed by the thought that a name change might make a difference.

'Okay, enough chatter now,' said Mrs M. 'Vira has an early flight to catch. Let's get dinner served. Now, look at these onions. Would a daughter of mine cut them so thick for the salad? I don't know why you do that.'

'Sorry, Amma,' the girl murmured. She held her bag up to the light as she retreated, repeating, 'Look, Akka, look how they shine.'

Mrs M was probably the only one to whom Vira could say, 'I think I am pregnant, and I don't want the baby.' And Mrs M was the only who would say, 'Nonsense, of course you do.' But Vira was leaving tomorrow, and there had not been a moment when Mrs M hadn't been surrounded by a flurry of home management. Vira hated the girl for being constantly present.

∞

The rains were long over, and it was the peak of the dry season by the time Vira sat at Mrs M's dining table six months later. The dust that must surely have been cleaned off only that morning had settled again on the table.

Vira doodled in the layer of gritty grey-brown as she waited for Mrs M to emerge from the kitchen; everything she drew these days looked like a mother and child. Hastily she rubbed it off, ran a duster over the table and laid out two cotton tablemats. Even though it couldn't be, she felt as if she remembered the mats from her parents' household; it was the soft darkening of the light, she thought, that was making her melancholic, raising nostalgic visions of childhood.

Suddenly, Simi was there, exclaiming loudly, 'Akka! Look, here I am. Did you miss me? You looked for me, didn't you? I was with my Mohan's family today.' The girl's excited tones dissipated the illusion of warmth and safety, and Vira was flooded by familiar anxious tensions that tautened her veins.

Mrs M came rushing out of the kitchen. 'Ah, child, I thought I heard your voice,' she said, beaming. The girl leapt at Mrs M and hugged her, crying, 'Amma!'

'Oh, how silly you are, child.' Mrs M wiped a tear, shook her head at Vira and gesticulated as if to say, look at this.

Before Vira could respond, the girl dashed to her purple and yellow raffia handbag lying on the sofa, rifled through it and extracted a small, shiny item. 'New. A pendant. My Mohan's mother gave it to me this morning.'

What was the girl doing here, anyway? Why couldn't she stay with her family now that she had a husband? Vira felt her head might explode with the bitterness but she managed to say, 'You have a nice mother-in-law.' Mrs M's gaze, still blurred from the tears she was wiping from her eyes, sharpened at Vira's tone.

The girl's energy seemed to dampen at the statement. 'She's not my mother-in-law. Not yet. But soon. You'll

come for the wedding, won't you? Won't you, Akka?
You have to say yes. We are fixing the date. I promise.'

Hearing that the October plans for connubial bliss
had been postponed, Vira felt marginally less close
to spewing out a terrifying monologue of rage and
disappointment. Clutching the chair, she said, 'If I am
here, I will.'

Mrs M moved quickly towards Vira and sat her
down at the dining table. Taking another chair herself,
she said to the girl, 'Go make something for Virakka
now.'

'Shall I make tomato salad for you? With onions?'

The thought of the sharp, wet, acid bits cut by the
girl made Vira feel sick. 'No, no. Simi, come back, do
that later,' she called. She took a shiny pair of bangles
out of a plastic bag on the table. 'I got you something.'

Mrs M's expression changed to a combination of
pleasure and feigned annoyance. 'Really, Vira,' she
said. 'The child has enough already.'

'Is it from your place?' asked Simi as she reached for
the bangles. Instead of slipping them on, she examined
them, saying, 'Aieeo, we had this fashion last year
already. Now it's only single-colour enamel bangles.
That's what I am going to wear at my wedding –
different set for every outfit. Matching. We are fixing
the date for the wedding soon. You will come, won't
you?' She ran from the room calling, 'Wait, I'll show
you my outfit.'

As they sat together in silence, Vira remembered one of the few times Mrs M had spoken about her own loss. Her husband's monthly cheque had just arrived, a sleek, white, monogrammed envelope among the dog-eared bills. Mrs M's hands had been coloured by the beetroot she had been grating and had left a terrifying purple-red smudge on the ridged paper as she turned it over. 'Really, it was not his fault alone,' she'd said with a sigh. 'I wanted a daughter so badly, and when I couldn't have one, I couldn't bear him any more.' And the memory so transported Vira to that moment that the ragged beetroot mark that had stained the envelope seemed to float now in the air and transfer, in a sad and ugly smear, on to everything – the wall, the tablecloth, even the backs of Mrs M's hands.

Vira rose, overcome by the image, and started to speak. But she fell silent when she saw that the woman who had been her friend and foster parent was stroking the embedded creases out of the tablemat as if smoothing out the wrinkles and folds in the handloom cotton rectangle was the most important thing to do. Vira felt a return of the singular sympathy that had bound them. Surely Mrs M too was remembering a time when they'd each shared their pain with the other?

'That poor child,' said Mrs M. Vira straightened abruptly, as if she had been slapped. Did Mrs M think about nothing but the girl these days? 'They are trying to rid her of all the stains on her horoscope before she enters their home. To protect them from the ill luck she apparently carries ...'

Vira felt as if she were choking.

Mrs M moved her chair back with a sigh. 'She really needs to be with him, poor thing. She is desperate, just desperate. Any daughter of mine who wants to marry, if her husband doesn't have enough guts for her, I'd tell her to leave, to go as far away as she can. I would just let her go rather than see her suffer like this.'

Let her go, thought Vira. She's taking over. I can't even speak to you any more. *I am desperate.* Don't you see it, I am desperate. Her body felt as it were torn apart by the flight and the heat and the dust and the disruption of her sleep cycle. She wasn't sure if she would make the trip across the oceans to visit Mrs M again. She wanted to cry but knew that would be foolish.

Mrs M looked as if she too was going to cry. But she began to laugh, a deep sobbing laugh, as Simi ran in wearing a pink net outfit embroidered with masses of gold and purple velvet flowers, gilt jewellery glittering madly in the evening light. 'We will fix the date any day now, Akka. You must come. Promise?'

SHOULD I WEEP?

The principal walked into the room in the middle of the geography lesson and the class sprang to attention. 'Good morning, girls,' she said.

'Good morning, madam,' they replied.

The teacher began, hastily, to wipe out the sketch on the blackboard. Sunanda stared as the oxbow lake disappeared. Intestines made oxbow shapes, masses of waste snaking within vigorous, peristaltic walls. Like the river, bending past her classroom, so compacted with refuse that a bottle tossed on to it didn't sink. Did intestines exist singly, she wondered. Rivers did. You could have one river, one oxbow lake. Could you have one intestine?

'You may sit.' The principal adjusted her stiffly held sari, her tight, firm hairdo casting a grotesque shadow on the wall, as if a hunched being was suctioned to her head.

Sunanda shifted in her chair. Her oxbow bends were changing direction. She felt churned up, sick.

'Settle down, girls. There's something I have to tell you.' The principal cast her sharp eyes about the room. 'Mrs L, your biology teacher, died on the operating table last night.'

The shuffling and whispering, the faint scraping from the starched pleats of the girls' uniforms went still. And into the silence the geography teacher dropped the duster with a crash, triggering gasps from the girls. Hira burst into hysterical tears.

Should I weep, Sunanda asked herself. She didn't feel upset or sad. But, imitating the others, she lifted her hand to her mouth and gasped like they had.

Despite her efforts to behave like everyone else, the principal noticed her. 'Sunanda,' she said, 'your right shoe lace is undone.'

Sunanda looked down at her shoe and its trailing lace. There was a dark, corrugated imprint on the Blanco-whiteness of the lace – whose shoe was it from, she wondered – and its end had turned scruffy and brown. 'Didn't I point that out to you in the corridor this morning? It is one thing to act as if you cannot speak when you are spoken to, we have to accept that, but I will not excuse untidiness. Tie it. Now.'

The girls snickered. Sunanda bent to knot the lace. She was afraid they would see her panties with the line of dark that wouldn't wash out of the seams and the edges. None of the others secreted dark juices. They didn't know what it was like to feel their organs move and contort.

It was not as if she didn't want to speak, but ever since her ovaries had ripped open, a thick bell jar of slowness contained her. The only thing she could really feel was the cramping pain. She didn't need to pick up the bifurcating tubes within her and hold them, as she had held amphibian intestines in the laboratory, in order to sense them. No, her tubes were outlined in a deep ache that spiralled directly to the wall of her lower abdomen.

The principal was telling the class about the assembly that was to be arranged for Mrs L. Mrs L had taught them about bifurcating tubes, about ovaries and eggs and fertilization. 'You'll feel it every month, the thickness and the tension and the flow,' she'd said. Only Sunanda had known what she was talking about.

Mrs L had also taught them about intestines. They had opened up a frog. 'Pin it, pin its legs,' Mrs L had said, her large body flapping above the girls as they bent over the lab tables. 'Open the abdominal wall. Look, there, you can see the intestines.'

The frog's intestines were shinier than Sunanda had imagined – purple-red and fine and shiny. And when Sunanda touched the hot, slippery volumes, they jumped, warm and alive. She had leapt back with a start.

'It is dead, you silly girl. Don't leap about in the laboratory.' Mrs L's voice was gravelly, like a man's, and her protuberant stomach rose in convex glory under her breasts.

'She's a beer drinker,' the American girl who had spent three months in their school had proclaimed. Sunanda and the rest of the class had stared in incomprehension. 'Yeah, my mum tells my dad that beer makes the guts big. My dad's got a giant big gut.' The American girl's dad and Mrs L probably had more oxbow twists in their intestines than others, Sunanda thought.

When Sunanda had peeped into the lab the day they had dissected the frogs, there was a sack in the corner, smelling of ponds and the egginess of rotting vegetation. 'You are early. Come back after the recess,' Mrs L shouted out from her cubicle.

The assistant saw Sunanda staring at the sack. 'Frogs,' he said with his habitual leer. He scratched his crotch, picked up the sack and inverted it into a long glass jar. The frogs tumbled in, their limbs waving in random directions. He poured in a measure of chloroform from a brown glass bottle. As the fumes rose, he corked the tall glass jar. The frogs began to leap, a single-minded mass pushing the cork with snouts and forelimbs, screaming a shrill, desperate sound. Frogs are silent animals. The males croak when they seek a mate, but otherwise they are voiceless.

Sunanda knew that from her biology lecture. But these frogs were screaming their last breaths away in a terrible chorus as they tried to escape.

Mrs L probably hadn't screamed when they covered her face in chloroform. She would have counted backwards and forwards until she was too drowsy to use that gravelly voice. The blade would have been sharp, the gloved hands that sliced open her abdomen, precise. How had they managed to pin back those large, heavy muscles? They must have had to contort her arms and legs, wrestling atrophied shoulders and hips into submission. Had they lifted out the slippery mass of her twisting intestines? Was it full of waste, the pulped remnants of her thick, dry rotis and garlic chutney?

Sunanda could smell that garlic chutney now. It used to pervade the lab, and certainly had on that dissection day, pungent and tangy over the smells of frog and chloroform and formaldehyde. That day, Mrs L's stomach and breasts had pressed down as she leaned over Sunanda and pointed out the different organs. 'Those are the vocal cords,' she had said. 'Humans have them, too, although some of us, like Sunanda, stop using them.' She had laughed, exuding fumes, setting the entire class into a giggle as Sunanda stood, pressed between the frog's exposed intestines and Mrs L's twisting gut.

What had they done with Mrs L's insides? She had seen the peon toss the frogs out for the stray dogs after the lab class. The dogs seemed to know the timetable and waited in the ditch outside, growling over the remains. It was the pups that got the intestines, minuscule and stringy, dragging them off in the dust. Mrs L's intestines would be too large for the pups. Maybe her thick convoluted tube went to the big male with one eye who growled whenever Sunanda passed by. He would probably snarl and sink his teeth into the remains of Mrs L.

'I want each of you to write a sentence for the memorial assembly. Hira, you seem deeply affected by her death. You were one of her better students, so you may read it out.' The principal looked around the class as if gauging the effect of this announcement. The girls sat straight, waiting to be dismissed. 'You can relax now, girls. Cry if you want to.'

Sunanda made a strangled sound.

'Sunanda, did you want to say something? Would you like to make a comment?'

Frogs are silent creatures, Sunanda wanted to say. All the girls were looking at her.

'Yes, Sunanda,' the principal said impatiently. 'Do you have something to add?'

Air squeezed through Sunanda's vocal cords and rushed past the strips of vibrating tendon to resonate in her oral cavity, forcing open her mouth in a high-pitched scream.

THE EMBRYOTIC

The conversation centred around the achievements of the children – other people's children – of course, and my mother-in-law stared at me significantly. My husband was gone, I was living in my maternal home, and the connection between our families could have been severed. But the complexities in our bloodlines meant that my mother-in-law was a cousin of my mother and was invited to visit during family events. And visit she always did because any child I produced would carry my husband's family name and she wanted to be sure to lay claim to it. Unless of course I attracted another man in marriage, as my mother hoped I would by parading me in ridiculous outfits. Tonight it was a crustily embroidered raw silk kurta and shiny satin pants, lime green and baby pink like Oprah's Jaipur outfit that she'd seen on television.

The point is, without my child, my husband's name was lost from the world forever; so my in-laws were willing to ignore the question of who the father was. There were rules there too, of course. Rules I was not willing to accept. My aunt Kamakshi said I was a stubborn girl, too fussy. 'Just do it. Think of all the wealth your child would inherit from your husband's side.' What did she think – that, like Ambika and Ambalika, I would simply close my eyes or blanch and suffer the lecherous old men in the family who were hoping to live forever through me?

∽

If I couldn't fulfil my purpose and bear children, I had to at least help around the house, I'd been told. I was assigned to work in the kitchen after my family asked the cook, Girija, to leave when the boil on her hand grew as large as a plum – not one of those fruit that are small, thin-skinned and yellow with melting flesh and veined fragility, but a robust, dark, purple-red variety from the hills of the Punjab, tight and dense with a generous circumference. When the bump had first appeared on Girija's hand, we'd ignored it, thinking it was an aggressive insect bite, especially as it didn't seem to stop her from chopping and stirring at her usual pace. Then we went through an awkward phase, when we were discreet and pretended it wasn't there. But as the days went by, it became more prominent, until its ripe glow suggested that a colony of bacteria was more than likely active beneath the stretched skin of the protuberance.

'You can't send me away when I am sick,' she'd protested. Her body sagged with the pain and the illness. It was a body I had always admired for its dumpy, primitive, earth mother look – vigorous despite the fact that her organs seemed to be compacted uncomfortably into a foreshortened abdominal volume. 'How will I manage if you dismiss me?' Her protest was weak and the family was steadfast in its determination to avoid having her pustular secretions leak into our food. She was given a month's bonus and we bid her goodbye.

Over the next few days, I pretended to do the cooking. My efforts were an affront to the family culinary legacy but I was determined not to get sucked into a cycle of condiments and tamarind-based stews accompanying every meal. A dal turned out by the maid formed the staple. I made sure I garnished it just as people congregated at the table, so they assumed it was my cooking they were sampling; I didn't disillusion them. I also extricated various pickles and forgotten frozen items left by visiting cousins from North America, and managed to make the meals look more respectable than they were. But the inevitable happened: Kamakshi – why did it always have to be her? – got a frozen piece of carrot in her stew. 'What is this, ice? An ice carrot,' she exclaimed, her shrill voice rising. I was in disgrace.

There was little point in trying to convince the

family that they had not been violated by the 'stale' food they'd been eating. In reality, the traditional taboos played a minimal role in our daily lives. All of us, including Kamakshi, enjoyed eating out in places where nobody kept track of who touched the food and how fresh it was. But having a daughter of the family blatantly and shamelessly disregard the rules in the home kitchen was unacceptable.

∞

That afternoon, I went to see Girija. Her hand looked like an inflated balloon. She sat cross-legged on a small stool, her hand resting, palm down, on her knee. The smooth, thickened, red bubble seemed almost to pulsate. I stared at it, fascinated. Girija looked resigned, as if she were getting accustomed to being the object of curiosity.

Ashamed of gawking, I tore my eyes away and looked around for a place to sit. There was no other furniture in the room. A small rag rug lay against the wall next to the door. I couldn't make out if it was a foot wipe or a mat on which to sit. She indicated the floor with her good hand but didn't offer the stool, as she ought to have to a guest. I remained standing.

'My husband is at work. I cooked for him this morning,' she said. An aluminium pot sat on the kerosene stove in the blackened kitchen corner. I doubted if, in her current condition, she could stir the

thick mixture of ragi and water with a steady enough
rhythm to ensure the sludgy porridge congealed into
the dense sphere of starch I knew her family favoured.
As if reading my mind, she said defensively, 'I can stir
the mudde with my left hand when it's still watery. I
only stop when it really begins to thicken. He says he
doesn't mind the lumps.'

I knew her husband was probably intolerant of
lumps and must have moved in next door with his
other 'wife', a young niece of Girija's who was about
sixteen. But I nodded. 'Have you eaten?' I asked.

'Ratni brings me something after he leaves. She's
a good girl.' Girija was the one who had 'procured' –
as Kamakshi so unambiguously phrased it – her niece
Ratna as a second wife for her husband when, after
a few years of Girija's marriage, no children had
appeared.

'Have you seen a doctor?' I pointed at her hand.

Girija shook her head. 'Ratni brought some herb
oil from the village. She applies it for me every day.'
The thick green-brown fluid in the reused Old Monk
bottle near the stove looked foul.

I shifted my feet, my stomach churning, and said,
'Let me take you to Dr Seshadri.' When Girija protested
that the oil was good enough, I told her, 'You can use
the oil too. He won't stop you.'

∽

Dr Seshadri's waiting room was packed. I flipped through an old *Femina* and read Maureen Wadia's advice to toned young beauty contestants as Girija dozed next to me, head drooped over her Willendorf-Venus body. I sat on her left, on the far side, that is, from her boil. She rested her suffering hand in the good one, both cushioned tenderly in her lap. The injured extremity looked like a small, hairless, juvenile animal, alive yet vulnerable.

The doctor looked surprised to see me. 'I thought you weren't in town,' he said. He was referring to my recent attempt to get away from the family. It had been a reaction to the pressure to produce an heir. He must have been the only one who missed the news that I had been retrieved from the mountain resort where I had fled. From what I could tell, the rest of the town had consumed my return with scandalous pleasure.

'Well, doctor, not only can I not bear children, I can't feed the family either. These are the only two duties that have been asked of me so far and I have failed. Do you think I should leave again?'

He told me not to be dramatic and asked Girija to show him her hand. She extended her arm towards him. 'She too hasn't had children and she's been married as long as I have. Did you know that?' I asked the doctor.

He ignored me and gently pressed Girija's wrist. She moaned and the balloon seemed to grow larger. I started back against the wall, fearing it would burst. The nurse came in and they gave Girija a shot in the arm. She slumped over instantly.

'Don't let her collapse. I can't cook, I need her!' I said to Dr Seshadri.

He continued to minister to her. 'An embryotic,' he said to the nurse, who nodded and inserted a giant needle attached to a tube into the boil. Gummy stuff flowed into a steel basin. I could feel my tongue beginning to glue to the top of my mouth at the sight. I swallowed quickly and said, 'She *can* cook, even if she, like me, can't produce children.'

Girija sat up and said, 'I can. I can produce children!' She tried to thrust her arm forward, became aware of the procedure it was going through and screamed, 'My baby, my baby!'

Dr Seshadri clucked angrily and held her arm down, saying, 'Calm down, you stupid woman. Look what you've done – I am going to try and transfer it.'

Over Girija's hysteria, I watched while the fluid level in the open lesion went down. It was quite magical: the skin on her hand crumpled and fell back like the petals of some dark, exotic flower to reveal a minuscule creature curled up on a dew drop-like bubble of thick shimmering liquid. Even Girija fell still and as we looked at its perfection together, I felt a great tenderness rise within me.

'I will have to work fast,' the doctor said.

Within seconds, the creature was scooped into a round glass vessel that had been warming to blood temperature in an incubator, or so the flashing display indicated. The nurse gently syringed the viscous harvested liquid down the sides of the bulb until the creature was floating in it. 'The safest would be a C-section insert,' the doctor said.

'You mean you are going to put it inside her?' I asked. Dr Seshadri knew my fascination with things medical and used to allow me to sit in on minor procedures in the days when I was contemplating becoming a doctor.

'It's small enough – let's try it without incision,' he continued to the nurse.

Without incision could only mean through an orifice ... the idea made me feel as if my insides were being invaded and I doubled over, clutching my stomach.

'Get her out of here,' he said. I fled to the waiting room but on the way I flicked a small drop of the embryotic gel from the basin on to my finger and stuck it in my mouth. It tasted oddly salty. Maybe it would seep into my system and line my uterus with nutritive layers so that, if I did conceive soon, my baby would be able to feed from the earth mother.

⁓

Seven months later, Girija's baby was born. She brought it home to show it off. It was minute and dumpy looking. I could imagine it growing up to be a compact male version of her. 'I can't come and cook in your house any more,' she said with a grin. I wanted to stomp and throw cold water on the limpet that clung to her breast.

'Maybe now *she* will be convinced it's time to have a baby,' Kamakshi said, gesturing at me.

How was I to tell her that I was more than convinced, even if my body apparently wasn't?

When I went to Dr Seshadri again, I told him, 'I've given up on cooking. Actually, I've been banished from the kitchen after my poor performance.' He once told my mother he never knew which past conversation I was going to dive into when I went to see him. I wasn't sure if she was pleased or embarrassed by his comment. He waited. 'I need to know how Girija achieved that baby,' I asked. 'Whatever it was, I think I'll do it too.'

'No, I don't think you will,' he said. 'It is unsafe, and you know it.'

'But you know I can make a baby. The ones my husband fathered simply didn't want to stay in my stomach. Maybe because my sense of food isn't up to family standards.'

'Just wait, you are young yet. It will happen,' he said, calling for the next patient who appeared at the door looking contorted and miserable. I paused, wondering what her problem was and why she was more deserving of the doctor's attention than I, but the receptionist led me out, saying, 'Come, come. It's nothing interesting – just constipation.'

Well, if Dr Seshadri wasn't going to help me, I'd have to find someone who would. I went to see Girija but she had no time for me. My mother told me not to be silly when I asked her if she knew how Girija had come about her child. 'Such things are unseemly. They aren't meant for people like us,' she said as she laid out the pink and green outfit and asked me to concentrate on the beauty routine she had prescribed for me.

∽

I slipped out of the house, escaping from the party conversation, feeling conspicuous in shiny raw silk and satin. As I began to walk towards the gate, trying to decide where on my body I would grow my baby and recognizing that nature had been wise in choosing the womb as the repository, my husband called out to me. What was he doing standing behind a tree on the driveway? There was a woman with him – a short, dumpy woman. Had he brought a new bride back from some other world? Maybe she was pregnant and the family would finally leave me alone, and I could try to sustain a baby, or learn to stop thinking about it and become a doctor or a scientist.

The balcony doors opened and I could hear Kamakshi saying, 'Where's she gone now, just when we are ready to introduce her to ...?' and my mother replying, 'Let her be ...'

The voices faded as the doors closed. Night surrounded us, quiet and warm. My husband smiled. As I moved towards him, I realized the woman with him was Girija. She held a ceramic pot in her hand, one of those dark, gritty ones that bonsai growers favour. In it was a plant, a succulent. Sprouting directly from its woody stem were dark, purplish-black flowers resembling the one I had seen on Girija's hand when the doctor had cut back the skin. Their petals were shiny and vigorous, ready to extend and reveal their interiors.

'For you,' she said, thrusting it into my arms. 'He wanted me to give it to you.' I was tempted to stroke the swollen petals but was afraid I might damage them.

Before I could ask Girija how fragile it was, how I should take care of it, whether I had to water it, and most importantly, which of the flowers would be most likely to be an embryotic, she said, 'I have to go now. You think now that I have a baby I can hang around with you whenever I want? I have things to do, unlike you.' Her teeth gleamed as she added, shaking her head smugly, 'So much work, you don't know what it's like.'

I carried the plant back to my room. As I walked through the front hall, it seemed as if the world had begun to change already. My relatives stepped back, my mother began to gasp and wail, and Kamakshi thrust a bottle of oily green fluid at me, saying, 'Try the thigh.'

I ignored them all and went up the stairs to my room. When I had changed out of the despicable clothes, I looked at the plant. I had to find the right soil in which to nurture it. I didn't want it on my body; it was not meant for people like us. But as I lifted the pot to take it down to the garden, it seemed the whorl of petals in the middle of the topmost flower shifted, drawing me towards it, and unfurled ever so slightly as if to reveal its centre.

IN 1997

When Ivana exited Bombay airport, it was raining hard. Scores of people stood on the outer perimeter of the metal fence that separated the arrival lounge from the zone where the public was allowed. Although the awning extended over the waiting people, it protruded only a few feet and was high over their heads. With every gust of wind, the monsoon waters lashed into those whose eyes eagerly scanned the grimy glass sliding doors, drenching their bodies and whipping their hair and clothes around them so they could not see and were themselves barely recognizable. Ivana wondered if anyone ever ended up leaving the airport with the wrong host.

She herself didn't have to worry about identifying a face. Instead, she had to identify her own name that she had been told would be inscribed on one of the A4-sized placards that the staff from the hotels were trying to hold steady in the wind. Ivana S. She liked using her initial to indicate her paternal lineage as, she had discovered, people did in some parts of south India. It was not the charm of it, however, that had convinced her to do so, but pragmatic reasoning: her surname was too complicated for her to spell out over a long-distance phone call and she didn't want to use Max's any more.

She wheeled her shaky luggage trolley to the metal fence, running over the potholes in the concrete with an anticipatory pleasure about the uncertainties that lay ahead.

'When do you get to the village?' Max had asked her from the next room when she was packing.

Given his increasing deafness that he would never admit to, she knew he hadn't heard her mumbled answer. She had been busy zipping her slick new folding bicycle into its special padded case, a task that needed her concentration, and was happy that his interest was minimal. Her ticket was valid for three years – a special deal worked out by her travel agent friend. She and Max were seeking separate paths now. It was time for her to find her happiness.

∽

'You said you were with her on the plane. Did you see her after you came out of immigration?' The investigator, whose name was Severin – although everyone who was not from the consulate pronounced it Swearin – did not wait for an answer but bent down and began to search noisily in his knapsack, mumbling to himself as he did so. The woman he was questioning stared, then turned away, and the accompanying official from the consulate looked anxious.

It had been three years since Ivana's disappearance from the airport, and the people who had been in the same cabin as her had been interviewed so many times that they had their stories honed down to the word. Severin's question was meant, therefore, not to gain new insights but simply to start the conversation. But as soon as he put the question to the woman with her dark brown, wide-pored, greasy skin and large accusing eyes, he was overcome. He felt that if he heard the woman's voice, he would be so repulsed, he would have to die immediately.

He straightened, extricating a worn notebook and pencil from the knapsack, opened the book and wrote down the number two on it. 'Two,' he said, and fell silent. Two people, he thought.

The sun played on the Formica table in the school hall in which they sat. The steel chairs that had felt pleasantly cool to the skin when they first arrived were now at body temperature and seemed almost clammy. Severin recognized it was his body that was generating the humidity and not the metal of the chair. They were perturbing the rhythm of the day. It was already that time of the afternoon when people unglued themselves from the surfaces they were sitting on and reposed on cotton sheets in the shade.

The others watched Severin, apparently waiting for him to speak. The whirring of the fan was the only thing that could be heard until a vendor with a cart called out, a long incomprehensible series of vowel sounds. Presumably he signalled positive enough things to those who understood his call that they aroused themselves from their post-prandial stupor to examine his wares.

This was the smallest of the places the investigation team had travelled to, and until this moment nothing of its character had particularly impressed itself upon Severin's mind. In fact, he had been in so many towns now that it was difficult to tell them apart. One of his tricks for remembering the different locations was the face of the accompanying consulate official and his or her expression during the trip. Most of them were frightened by the fact that they had been transported out of the familiarity of the city, but they responded in individual ways. This man was a shrinker; he shrank into himself, cloaking himself in his anxieties.

A boy brought in chai. He plonked down the glass tumblers of the fragrant hot liquid, then stood and stared at the consular official.

'What is it?' the man asked after a minute or so. He wiped his spectacles with a checked kerchief that he took from his jacket pocket and scrunched his face up to stare at the boy.

'Paisa?' the boy said, rubbing his fingers together and lifting his chin inquiringly.

The man drew the checked cotton square across his face, laid it on his khaki trousers, then took out a few rupees from a wallet that he held close to his chest.

The boy returned a five-rupee note, and the man perspired some more and waved his fingers, saying, 'Take it, take it.'

'Is he scared?' the boy asked the woman in Tamil. The woman grinned and opened her mouth as if to respond, and Severin got up and walked quickly out of the room.

After making confused and mollifying sounds, the official staggered out behind Severin.

There was a sheltered bus stop outside the school with a large tree next to it. Severin stood under the tree and pushed his hair back with one hand. 'It's time,' he said, 'to head back to the city.'

At the consulate, Severin told the consul general, 'There is no point in continuing the investigation in this way. I gain nothing from travelling to all these towns asking worn-out questions to fellow passengers of Ivana Starcikowska. We have to find out why.'

'What do you mean, "why"?'

They spoke in English, not their native language, having fallen into the habit since they often had to discuss the case in the presence of local people who needed to follow them. The consul general's accent, particularly in a tongue foreign to him, was slow and mincing, which allowed the trailing sound of the 'why' to linger and fade, and for the quiet to settle into the room. Severin listened and waited instead of thundering in to answer as he might normally have. Eventually he said, 'Why she came back here in the first place.'

'Why she came here? To India? But we know that – a cycling trip, no?' The consul general's fair, bovine face looked confused. Even his fine fair hair seemed to move questioningly as his eyebrows rose and his brow furrowed.

Severin did not say, 'We want to know why she really came back to India, what she was looking for ...' Neither did he admit that his increasing reluctance to ask questions of people whose recollections were fuzzy and coloured by suggestion was beginning to manifest itself in an unbearable nausea. He simply nodded.

When he was first asked to look for Ivana, he had said, 'Who was she? You see, that's what we need to know. Then we might be able to determine what she did when she came out of the airport. Did she get to the wrong hotel, did she sleep in Bombay, did she leave? That will help us find out what happened to her. Whether she died, was killed, was kidnapped, chose to disappear ...'

Now, after all these months of searching for her, he felt he was no closer to the answer of 'who' but was pressed by the question 'why'. Why did Ivana return to India?

∽

When Ivana was a little girl, she had longed to travel to India. Her father had given her a magazine on the cover of which was a photograph, set in a gamboge yellow border, of a woman with a bright veil over her head. And when she opened the magazine, a rich, full, other world was revealed. Ivana had imagined herself becoming beautiful and being part of the pictures. By the time she went to India for the first time, she knew she would never be beautiful. She was not perturbed, therefore, by the fact that the place did not look like the magazine pictures with their marble arches and vivid, wild colours. She could accept the grime and the poverty and the begging children. 'I want to really get to know the people,' she told everyone she met. 'I must travel in India by bike so that I can really go everywhere, stop anywhere.' She would nod in emphasis as she spoke.

∽

In 1997, Severin had come to India with a college friend whom he had lost track of. His memory of the visit was foggy: heat, inebriation and a hallucinatory glow veiled the misery of discovering that his birth mother, whom he had traced from the papers his adoptive parents had left, was either dead or a beaten-up Goan whore with no interest in him. His stomach had given in to tropical flora and fauna, and his college friend had left him in a local hospital and gone on to Kathmandu.

Now Severin was discovering that Ivana's first visit to India had also been in 1997 and that she had been in the very same hospital as he had, most likely at the same time, for an injured toe. He knew this from notebooks in which she had maintained a diary. The books had only recently been sent to him, having been discovered in a cupboard by her ex-husband, Max. Max had reported her missing after these many years when he found he needed her permission to sell some joint property they owned. 'Either she must sign or be declared dead or officially missing,' Max said when agreeing to Severin's fee.

In the diary, Ivana had written, 'That nurse Jayashree leers at me even when she is dressing my toe. The doctor says the infection is gone. I can leave tomorrow.' The entry was marked May 1997. A few undated notes followed. On 6 June she had written, 'oh dear god, oh dear god. so incredible am i crazy?' Her handwriting seemed to be more alive, less controlled, conveying an excitement – a joy, almost? Severin chided himself for reading too much into the statement and told himself it might have been sex or drugs, not love, that had driven her to write it.

He remembered that in June 1997 he had finally begun to feel a sense of hope about himself. When the nurse who had processed his discharge forms said 'Go well', he had felt strength in his body. Even though it was hot and humid, he had gone straight from the hospital to the sea and sat on the sand at the edge of the water, the waves washing over him. Hypnotized by the movement, he'd decided to give in to the draw of the sea and let it take him where it would. He lay down flat, just where he was. Warm liquid lifted him, and he could hear a million things rushing over his body. But he could breathe – he was still at the surface and could breathe.

When the water eventually receded, he found he was only a few feet away from where he had been. He wiped the salt and sand delicately from his lids and opened them. A girl was smiling down at him, shading the sharp circle of the sun and surrounded by a halo of light. The water droplets that clung to his lashes reproduced her image multiple times. The psychedelic effect dissipated as he raised himself, and she sat down beside him. They looked out at the horizon together until the sun set. Then, she held his hand and led him to her room. She had not spoken and neither had he. And she had not stopped smiling. He didn't know her name and was not even sure he remembered her face.

But he could remember, with incredible glory, the joy of it.

∽

Severin made use of the consulate's connections to trace Ivana's nurses. They found Jayashree. She was from Kerala and had found a job in Dubai in 1998 but had returned recently to work in a hospital in the city.

She was about to start the day's duty when he went to see her. Her fat, round face creased with suspicion. 'Investigator? I don't have to return any money. The Dubai agent is fully paid and I am not owing anyone else.' That was the trouble with looking like he did not belong, Severin thought. People assumed, not without reason, that he was low down in some bureaucratic hierarchy. Severin explained that he was not interested in her money but was looking for a woman who had been in her care.

'In 1997?' She opened her eyes wide in incredulity.

'Yes, 1997,' Severin asserted.

She laughed.

He had requested but had not yet received photographs of what Ivana had looked like then. He had nothing to show Jayashree and began, therefore, to try and describe Ivana and her injured toe, when a woman in a crushed cotton sari, holding a brown cardboard file, hurried up and said, 'Gynaecology, please. Urgent.' Jayashree pointed to a staircase. They were interrupted a second time by a nurse who came up and began to discuss a patient with Jayashree, apparently oblivious to the fact that he was talking to her.

Before Jayashree could be distracted once more, Severin took her elbow and said, 'Canteen?' She shook off his hold and wiped the spot he had touched with her other hand, but led the way down the stairs to the basement.

The canteen was relatively empty. The light from the windows that were high up on one wall was cloudy and dull. The electric lights in the room, barring the one above the serving counter, were switched off. When Severin asked why it was so dark, the man who served them explained that economy dictated that they leave the lights off outside the peak serving hours.

Severin got two cups of tea. He opened his mouth to ask Jayashree a question, then took a quick gulp of the sweet scalding beverage to still the tightening of his stomach.

'I remember, I remember!' she exclaimed suddenly. 'Foreigner. Very tall. Big face. Ugly. Injured toe? Yes, yes. I remember because when she came for last dressing, she was sitting on the examination bed, I was on a stool and she said, "Look up, look at my face. See my happiness." So I looked up from her foot from which I was removing the bandage and she had a big smiling happiness. I never saw ugliness go away like that before. That's why I remember.'

Severin put his head between his legs. The nurse rubbed his neck, then made him sit up and take another sip of his hot, sweet tea. She continued to talk. 'It was 1997, correct. Must be June. Because July I went to my native place and September, I left for Dubai.'

At the mention of Dubai, her face, which had taken on a sort of glowing eagerness as she recalled the Ivana story, creased like the skin of a fruit gone past its prime. 'Okay, I am late. I must go,' she said, and left.

∽

When Ivana went for a walk that day, it felt almost like she had never walked before. Her muscles had become accustomed to the life of a wealthy, urban Indian – overfed, sedentary and transported by car wherever she needed to go. Many people in her current circle, including the woman who had decided Ivana was so much like her dead daughter that she wanted to keep her, had a certain massiveness, a density of flesh, a rippled thickening, that suggested an even more solid packing of tissue and fat below the surface. They reminded her of her East European relatives from previous generations who ate with gusto and suffered from gout. Not at all like her stringy, hungry contemporaries. She could not judge if she too were becoming thicker and if her ankle joints also had a genetic tendency to fill with toxins and cease to function if she remained inactive.

She had woken up three years ago after a fall on the wet airport tiles to find she did not even remember her name. Her tongue was accustomed now to spice and complexity, but every now and then she would yearn for the stolid white blandness of her childhood. At first, taste was her only recollection of a past life. Now, she could name all her European relatives and detail her relationships with them. She did not reveal that to anyone, not even to the kind family that had taken her in and tried to mould her into one of them, because she was still not sure who she really was. But she knew she had to find out, because even during the worst of her fog she had not forgotten that she had come here on a search. A search for happiness.

She dug her toes into the sand, revelling in its grittiness, and could feel memories of texture and of mobility awakening. After two hours of walking, there was a pace to the bending of her knees, a rhythm of stretch and contract that reassured her that her body still functioned. She felt as if some core of her was being released from layers of another life. Her lungs filled with air and she smiled.

At the far end of the beach, a large vehicle pulled up. A man got out, a big man, who extended his arms wide. Was he stretching, was he raising his arms to the heavens, was he holding them open for her, was he going to snatch her away from her search? Ivana stumbled and fell in the sand.

∽

Severin walked slowly. The tide was going down and the water was receding, abandoning minute cockleshells on the sand. He remembered the girl picking up handfuls of them and tossing them back in the water. He could not remember her face any more, but the memory of her smile was like a bright light in his being. His stride lengthened and he felt a sense of urgency course through him. At the other end of the beach, a woman fell in the sand.

Severin began to run towards the woman as fast as he could.

SHE CAN SING

Mrs Sen's palms felt soft and smooth and a little pudgy to the child as they cupped her face. They made her think of Pink Doll. She missed Pink Doll.

It had been busy at the intersection under the overpass; there were lots of big cars on the afternoon she'd found the doll. The traffic light had started to flash prior to changing when a cotton-candy rainbow came arcing across the grey and landed on the road. She'd darted out from Poorvi's hold, picked it up and run back, clutching the woolly head, accompanied by the other kids' shrieks of 'hurry, hurry', only to have Raji snatch at the doll's brilliant pink hair and yell, 'It's mine, I saw it first. Give it to me.'

'Let her have it, you cow!' Poorvi shouted and yanked Raji away. 'Kid doesn't have anything, not even a name. Let her keep the damn doll.'

Raji let go but bared her teeth and jeered, 'Anaamika'.

The child hadn't cared that she was being labelled 'the nameless one'. When she closed her eyes now, she could remember what it had felt like to stand in the shadow of the massive concrete arches, hugging the doll to her chest.

The sensation evaporated as Mrs Sen removed her hands, leaving a shallow vacuum around her face.

'Sangeeta, that's what I'll call you,' Mrs Sen said. 'Yes, Sangeeta, music – that will be your name. And I will teach you to use that voice of yours.'

❧

Sangeeta quickly learnt that she was expected to be properly dressed for the daily singing lesson. 'Not finished plaiting Sangeeta's hair yet?' Mrs Sen would snap at Radhabai who had been assigned to care for her. Or, 'What kind of crushed skirt is the child wearing, Radhabai? Iron not working?'

But even more important than the state of her appearance was whether her voice was ready. Sangeeta was expected to have her voice warmed up before the early morning class.

Once, when she overslept, Mrs Sen said fiercely, 'I didn't hear you practise today.' She had extended her neck as she spoke, and drawn her eyelids back, so her eyes looked round and fierce like those of the dragons outside the Chinese restaurants.

Sangeeta cringed. But Mrs Sen didn't yell or raise

her hand as angry people had done in Sangeeta's past. Instead, she prepared for the lesson, settling down cross-legged on the mat and arranging her sari. But rather than tuning her tanpura as she usually would, she said in a tight, cold voice, 'Don't ever enter my music room without your voice ready. You'd still be in the sewer but for your god-given gift. Practise, or I'll toss you back as easily as I snatched you from that hell. Now sing.'

⁂

It was the doll that had first brought Sangeeta's song to life. To stay away from Raji's taunts, she'd used a torn bit of sari and a piece of thermocol to build herself a shelter against the concrete columns of the overpass. Hidden inside, she would try to wipe off the dust and the grime of the exhaust fumes from the doll and brush its woolly hair back with her fingers. And she would sing, her voice opening up and exploring unmapped tunes.

One day, when she was in her shelter, she heard a slap. 'Where's that other kid, you bitch? You have seven in your group but I see only six.' Careful not to draw attention to herself, the child peeped out as a scarlet spurt of paan juice landed on the grit. A pair of dirty white bell-bottoms, tight on a skinny frame, stepped over the spit blotch that stood out, bright and opaque. It was the 'boss'. 'Make your quota or fucking see what happens. Do you want me to send you out with the whores?' he snarled as he headed off.

As soon as he had gone, Poorvi dragged the child out, knocking down the tenuously attached bit of thermocol. 'I should have given you up to the bastard,' she said, running her fingers over the ugly welt on her cheek. 'Stop playing with that stupid doll and go bring in the money.' She reached for the toy, but when the child crouched and whimpered, she said, 'All right, don't look so frightened. I won't take it away. But do the job or he'll hurt me and then hurt you.'

The child scurried out, tapping on car windows. 'Eat, I need to eat,' she whined, holding out the doll as she'd seen Poorvi and the others do with the babies they collected every morning. 'Eat, hungry, eat.' It was the first time she had used the doll when begging. One or two people laughed but nobody gave her anything.

'Sing, you idiot!' Poorvi yelled.

Standing close to a silver-grey car, the child began to sing, her voice rising. On the other side of the tinted glass, a little girl with a curly head of hair screamed and pointed. A lady lowered the window, and cool, scented air hit the child's face.

'My doll, Mummy! My pink doll – look.'

'Shh, don't shout so, sweetie, you'll scare the child,' the lady said. Her fingers moved rapidly over her telephone. The curly haired girl kept up a high-pitched screech and reached for the pink doll. Petrified, the child continued to sing, holding the doll close. The lady spoke into her telephone. 'Hi, Mrs Sen, you won't believe … among the beggars at the flyover … an angelic voice …'

*

'No, not orange, we mustn't clash on stage. Wear the green silk,' Mrs Sen said as she unlocked a cupboard and took out a skirt and blouse from a multi-coloured array. She held them up against Sangeeta who raised her toes to feel the cool heaviness of the gold border on the full skirt. The clothes smelled of cloves and star anise. 'Good,' Mrs Sen said. 'I thought they would fit.'

She took out a pair of emerald earrings from a drawer and held them out to Sangeeta: 'Put these on.'

Sangeeta fumbled with the stems of the fine green stars and Mrs Sen bent impatiently to help. Her plump fingers were surprisingly agile, fitting and turning the screws efficiently. But then, they lingered, gently following the contours of Sangeeta's ear lobes. As if in a trance, Mrs Sen sat down and touched Sangeeta's face, enclosing the child's cheeks with her palms even more tenderly than she had that first day. Sangeeta thought Mrs Sen might even hug her and wondered what that would be like. But then Mrs Sen shook her head, as if breaking out of a spell, and stood up, covering her eyes with her hands.

'Go,' she said, and her voice trembled. 'Take your

blessings from Goddess Saraswati for your first time on stage. Go.'

∞

'You did well, child.' Mrs Sen smiled. But Sangeeta felt as if Mrs Sen was talking not to her but to someone else. She stood back quietly against the wall as Mrs Sen opened her supari case, sorting and mixing the delicate, striped shavings of betel nut with cloves and cardamom. As admirers began to gather at the entrance of the green room, she said, without even turning her head, 'Radhabai, take her away. Now.'

At the stage exit, Sangeeta sensed that people were looking at her. She knew Mrs Sen would expect her to greet them, but she stared instead at a yellow moth that spiralled outwards from the street lamp. A woman said, 'Look, there's the child, so young.' 'Oh, don't go talk to her, darling,' someone else responded. 'Don't you know, she's terrified of people, barely speaks.' 'Really? Extraordinary! Miracle that Mrs Sen found her,' a third person said.

'Not Mrs Sen!' The tone was indignant. '*I* found her. Last year, at the overpass before the highway turn-off.'

Sangeeta glanced over quickly. It was the lady from the car, the mother of the curly haired girl. She was looking around triumphantly as she nodded and continued, 'I rang Mrs Sen immediately and held my phone out the car window. Even through the racket of the traffic and my daughter's screams, she could hear that voice, pure and clear.'

Sangeeta hunched her shoulders and looked down at the ground.

'Do you know,' the lady continued, 'she snatched the child off the street the same day? It wasn't easy, literally a tug-of-war. The street children hung on to the kid. Then, as they lost their hold, they hung on to her doll, and when that too slid out of the child's fingers, they ran after the car, holding up the doll. And you know the craziest coincidence? The doll, it was my daughter's pink one that she'd thrown out of the car weeks before in a tantrum! Isn't that a wild story?'

'Mrs Sen tells everyone the child is a relative. To think she's just a casteless orphan from the streets!'

'Come on, what does it matter where she comes from? It's her voice that counts!'

'True. First time I've heard such purity of tone after Mrs Sen's daughter. Such a tragedy, that.'

'Yes. During childbirth, in this day and age! How Mrs Sen must feel.'

'Especially since *she* was the one who drove her out. She knows the girl might have survived had she kept her at home. Wonder what happened to the baby.'

The warm blanket that Sangeeta hadn't even known she'd drawn around herself over the past months seemed to disappear. She held herself tight, as if she were hugging Pink Doll.

Mrs Sen's car drove up. The yellow moth smashed into the windshield, spreading fine dust on the glass.

'Come, come, why are you shaking now? Get in the car, don't dawdle,' said Radhabai, taking Sangeeta's arm and hustling her in.

'Shouldn't you sit in the back with her?' the driver asked Radhabai, who ignored him and settled into the front. Their chatter washed over Sangeeta as she lay back on the seat, arms around herself, looking out at the passing lights.

'Eat, hungry, eat.'

With a start, she sat up. It was Poorvi, small and shrunken. She held a sleeping baby whose limbs flopped like those of a badly stuffed toy.

Sangeeta lowered the window. Poorvi fell silent. They reached for each other's fingers.

'What's wrong with you? Can't you see the AC is on? You want to cool the whole world or what?' Radhabai snapped.

The driver pressed a button and the window began to rise. The child kept her fingers on the edge but Poorvi withdrew hers and fumbled among the rags at her waist. Just before the gap closed, she tossed something into the car.

'What was that? Throw it out. Throw it out!' Radhabai shrieked and scrabbled behind her seat, but when she couldn't find anything, her attention returned to the film song that was playing on the car radio.

Sangeeta took a grubby sphere out from under the folds of her silk skirt. It was the pink doll's head, squashed and dirty, its broken neck protruding. She could just make out its features in the passing bands of neon. The woolly hair was sparse now, an indefinable colour, but when she stroked it, she felt as if she could see its original pink fluorescence.

She closed her eyes and began to sing. And as she did, her fingers ran tenderly over the doll's neck that, severed from its body, was open and reaching – as if trying to find a place to attach to.

THE INSERT

They are inserting a piece of land between the seventh and eighth lanes that run off the main causeway in the south. That's where I live, in that bit of the city that squeezes away from straight lines and neat grids into a messy, crooked criss-cross. Rather like the squares we had to knit in school that lost and gained stitches and ended up as unexpected trapeziums; regardless of the original colour of the wool, my knitting always finished up a tight, tortured grey, not unlike the streets I am talking about.

But I shouldn't complain – my stretch of the street is, in fact, not as grimy as all that. The sidewalk is wide; it was redone only last year with interlocking blocks that fit together like a jigsaw and are smooth and not yet majorly sullied by smashed-in litter and indelible carmine paan splats. A few of the buildings have been recently cleaned and painted, and bear that better-than-new air that's characteristic of faraway

European cities. If you narrow your vision and ignore the grit in the interstices, you might think you were in a better part of town.

The digging began in the night. Usually the inserters start early, bold and uncaring of the sensibilities of the city, cordoning off sections of the sidewalk so schoolchildren have to edge past the seeping muck of severed drains to get to the bus stop. Whatever the devious reasons for starting after dark this time, it was certainly not to save us any inconvenience: the approaching machines were monstrous and loud, waking me up from a deep sleep. This was followed by the unmistakable sound of the earth tearing. Even if you've heard it before – the tight, shredding sound, harsh and resistant, like multiple layers of packed cardboard being ripped apart – it evokes terrifying images. Tonight, I was reminded of cartilage being separated under a cardiac surgeon's tools, whatever that might really sound like.

I rushed to my window. The street was bright with the light of giant petromax lamps. The claws of the machine were inserted between the slabs of the pavement and were just starting to cleave the ground. I could see the beginnings of the dark vacuum they were creating, an empty volume reaching deep into the bowels of the earth. On the surface, the empty space appeared triangular and impenetrable, a black hole reflecting back nothing. From where I stood, so high above the ground, I should not have been able to make it out, but the picture was so intense that the edges of the triangle seemed to be lined with flat, pale, polymer fibres, as if the earth had a tight supporting web stretched across it – a web that was reaching resolutely across the surface of nothingness to try and reconnect.

That surely was my imagination, piecing different pictures together and 'seeing' something that wasn't there. I wish the authorities could see how I was able to extend myself like that.

I wanted to run down to check if what I thought I saw was true, but remembered the time I'd been watching the machines near the middle of our park and how tempting it had seemed to fling myself into the void. It was one of the early big diggings when the city had begun to demonstrably fail in controlling the rise of the illegal real estate inserters and they were greedy and blatant in their activities. Now they have so much power, having insinuated themselves into the system, that there is an air of official industry about them, as if insertion is part of the routine civic maintenance in the city, even though everyone knows it is outside the law.

That day, a crowd had gathered in the park, some five or ten people at first, and then more jostling curiously behind. There were signs, yellow with bold black letters, alerting bystanders not to cross the tape. Despite the warnings, a man had gone beyond the boundary and got sucked into the vacuum. It happened so fast – the man tumbling awkwardly, arms pulled downwards, head too, legs splayed apart and bent at the knee and vibrating like a failed Olympic diver with palsy – that the child whose hand he had just let go had not even begun to open his mouth to scream before the man disappeared.

I had wanted to take the child with his china-doll face home, but the head of the digging operation grabbed him and, within seconds, the authorities had surrounded the child and swooped him away. I wondered then, and I wonder again now, what had induced the man, especially one with a child, to take that fractional step past the boundary. For I was next to him and saw that it was deliberate, what he had done. He'd let go of the child's hand and slid his foot forward, leaning his torso ever so slightly into the powerful force that lay beyond the invisible but discernible electromagnetic barrier.

So now, even though I was curious, I resisted going down to the pavement to see what the machines were up to and to check whether my mental image of the earth's binding web was real, because I was afraid I would be tempted to do the same as the man, for no other reason than to experience what it felt like to completely disappear.

By the morning, the point of the dig's triangle was edging towards my building. If it came too close, it would take part of the building away.

I was once driving on the big street that connected the city to the estuaries. Property was being appropriated by the city in order to improve the coastal road. The narrow dwellings that lined the road were being demolished to widen the thoroughfare. The homes looked as if they had been severed in half, sliced through, leaving neat brick-stepped walls to rise up from the debris and hold up the remains of the roofs.

I felt as though I were viewing a human-sized doll village with one wall removed. Every interior was a different colour: pastel pink, green, yellow, blue. Traces of people's daily lives had been left behind: a dark red cotton cradle slung across the room, strangely wrinkled and empty; a calendar image of an abandoned goddess, crooked on the wall, her multiple hands held up in skewed fury – or was it hesitant benediction? – her head partially ripped off and her vigorous colours covered in grey dust.

The road disintegrated into a pile of rubble on which sat an old lady in a dusty purple sari. I stopped and got out of the car.

'They found her in her house,' a man told me. He was bringing her a plastic cup of chai. 'Here, drink it.'

She turned to him with a bewildered air.

'Drink it,' he repeated loudly, bending to speak into her face. To me he said, 'She was my neighbour. Used to tell me stories when I was a boy.' He shook his head.

'We try to move her but she digs her fingers into the dirt and crawls back.'

All the time he was speaking, the old lady stared at him. Then, very slowly, as if she had finally managed to understand the connections between what he said and what was being asked of her, she began to raise one shrivelled, claw-like hand to reach for the tea.

When I had stopped my car, it had been to check if there was some way to navigate the rubble. But I couldn't do it, couldn't drive through her home, so I'd reversed back down the street until the turn-off. I don't think she noticed me at all.

I could not imagine how I would feel if my living space were to get carved into as invasively the old lady's had been.

By the afternoon, the vacuum triangle was touching my wall. When I opened my window, I could feel the air vibrating with the force of the energy wave that kept us all from being sucked into the depths. My wild hair aligned itself with the wave and turned into a broad brown-black ribbon that moved with a slow, Légeresque periodicity. I could feel my synapses getting affected; a lulled compliance to nothingness was washing over me.

It was time to get away or I could imagine myself succumbing to the void.

I shut the window quickly, grabbed my cat, put her in her basket, strapped it on around me and ran to the door. But before departing, I dashed back and moved the vase at the window to near the front door. The vase was Chinese, exquisite and old, and had belonged to my grandmother, or to hers. If my building did get touched, if the window did get opened up, I hoped that the vase would lie beyond the edge of the suction force and survive.

I spent the rest of the day in the park. The minute I edged open the lid of her basket to stroke her, the cat jumped out. It was her first taste of the outdoors. She leapt on to a branch with a grace and surety that evoked in me an unfamiliar protective feeling. But she was out of reach. Except for twitching her nostrils, she didn't move for what seemed like half an hour. Then she streaked into the undergrowth like a flash of lightning and disappeared from sight.

I called her a few times in a desultory way. She and I both knew our relationship was over, anyway. She had stopped coming to greet me when I got home, preferring to sleep by the window in the warmth of the sun during the day, and to watch the flashing lights of the city as she cleaned herself at night. And I too had ceased to rush to the windows to pet her the minute I entered the house, stepping more easily into selfish grooming routines of my own.

We were roommates now, not soul mates. Was that another sign of my failure to connect? Or hers?

Either way, now I sat on the bench and waited for

her. But then the lights came on in a building in the near distance, on the other side of the trees. I realised that it was the one that had been constructed on the first insert I had seen, the one that had emerged over the vacuum into which the man got sucked. Curiosity got the better of me, and I gave up waiting and went across the park to have a look at it.

I had never knowingly crossed inserted ground before, and I tried to step lightly, the image of the disappearing man in my mind. But my anxiety dissipated when I reached the front of the building – I was too distracted by the shining newness of it. Here I was, surrounded by my familiar, shabby park, but the gardens immediately fronting the building were neat and tamed – hedges trimmed, paths paved and lit.

A child emerged through the doors. It was unaccompanied but seemed to know it should not cross beyond the well-kept garden. It looked like the child who'd let go of the hand of the man who fell. A second child joined the first, also with the same perfect china-doll looks. What were they – clones of the abandoned child?

I waved out to them but they shrank back and a man stepped into the gardens, shouting, 'Get out!' Now my imagination was really working, for the man looked like the one who had fallen into the abyss.

'This is a public place,' I replied, even as I shrank into the bushes, stepping on empty packets of pan masala and slippery discarded condoms. Vile! I came out of the bushes quickly, scraping my slippers vigorously on the stone paving.

The man stood holding the children close. 'I remember you,' I called out.

'No. You are mistaken, I don't know you ...' His voice trailed off and he moved forward, one child grasping each hand. When I continued to stare, he said, 'I am not supposed to talk to you ... to anyone.' His voice shook. 'They promised me a second son, a replica, if I took part in their experiment.'

'Experiment?'

'You saw me – I went into the hole. But you didn't see that I was thrust back up to the surface. I could have been lost in the abyss, but I live.'

His fingers tightened on the children who stared at me. One of them began to cry. The man bent and whispered something to the child, then straightened and said to me, 'I can barely tell them apart now, except that the one who came after never cries.'

At close range, the man's skin seemed to be crossed by millions and millions of small lines. A little as if he had been under water too long, except the effect was dry and papery, and there were many, many more little troughs and peaks. He shook too. I assumed it was an effect of crossing the protective field with its strong vibrations, but he told me the palsy was his own. 'You see me? The trembling will get worse. This way the child will have someone to call his own.' He moved back to the building, whispering, 'Please go, please go.'

As I walked back through the park, I called out to my cat. She had been the metaphoric cloned child, my sole companion after my family was reassigned to another. I'll never forget that my daughter had wept when they had taken her away and I hadn't, and that the officials had used it as further proof of my incapability to love and empathize. I couldn't tell them that I was weeping inside.

Was I letting my cat go as well now? Did it mean I was healed, or did it mean that I was embedded in solitude? Initially, when I found myself alone, accused by the courts of 'lack of imagination', of 'cruelty arising from an inability to understand what other human beings feel', I had stayed in my flat, teaching my mind to be blank. Then I began to work – intense research into the molecular triggers for imagination and thus empathy. The work distanced me from my cat.

When I returned to my building, the machines were driving off. My street, which had been straight, now snaked around an island with a sharply angled construction directly in front of mine.

An expansion had been inserted into my building just as I had anticipated. My drawing room, which used to have narrow French windows, now had a wide, curved bay window that allowed me a view of the city beyond the corner of the structure in front.

The inserters had been kind and laid the same floor as the original, so the triangle leading from the bay window to the centre of the room was just a little darker, less faded. It gave the room a certain focus. I was not displeased. The workers had been fairly conscientious about clearing up the detritus of insertion and construction. There was an extra layer of dust over the old space, but no piles of cement or sand or wet mud.

I tidied up and brought the Chinese jar back to where it had been, and sat down in the cat's spot in the now expanded window.

Lights were coming on in the new building as people started to move in. There was a little girl on a rug on the floor. She might have been nine or ten. She looked like my little girl. She was playing with a cat. It was my cat. I hoped that soon the buildings would merge into one.

MY KITCHEN, MY SPACE

Mala's lungs emptied as if a sudden pre-monsoon pressure change had thrust itself densely into her diaphragm. She gasped and put the saucepan down on the stove with a sharp clatter. The wavefront enveloped her now, like a vice around her middle. Holding the counter, she turned with an effort to see what the cause of the tension was.

Her mother-in-law had entered the kitchen!

Light from the dining room silhouetted the old lady, outlining her body. But while her shoulders were held soft and she appeared to lean solicitously forward, her legs were firmly planted and her stance was territorial. My kitchen, it screamed. My saucepan!

Mala wished she weren't here, in this kitchen. She wished Saurav hadn't had to bring them – her and the children – here to his mother's place.

'It's just for a few weeks,' he'd said despairingly when the boarding school offered him a teaching job with no accommodation. The salary was pitifully low but he had no choice. 'Once I am there, I'll surely get housing, Mala,' he'd continued in a flat yet hopeful voice. 'Until then, why don't you move in with my mother?'

'We'll be fine by ourselves,' Mala tried to insist. 'You don't need to take us to your mother's place. My family will help me.'

'Your sister is dead, Mala,' he'd replied. Or had he said your mother is mad, your father is gone, your brother doesn't care. She couldn't remember precisely what he had said, nor what she had said. She only knew that on that day, neither of them could bear to acknowledge that they couldn't afford to keep their home any longer. A few weeks later, they had emptied out the house and sold most of their things.

And now, Mala thought, she didn't have a home. Nor, apparently, a saucepan in which to heat milk for the children's cocoa.

'I've told you so many times that we take out the new stainless steel saucepan only when we have guests. What don't you understand about that? Use *this* one for everyday – see, this one,' Saurav's mother was saying. She was holding out the grey aluminium saucepan with the crêpey Teflon interior.

Not the Teflon-coated pan, Mala wanted to say. The neutral flakes of the rubbery, indestructible polymer will enter my children's bodies. Resinous, elastic scales, eternally non-reactive, will lodge in my children's organs and accumulate in unknown crevices, making their sweet bodies obese and cancer-prone. Minute, non-stick bits, inorganic plankton, so small that they are invisible, will wash through my children's tender internal filters, and attach scrapings of my children's helpless, innocent cells to the swirling, giant sphere of plastic waste in the ocean.

'This one,' the old lady emphasized, tapping her fingers on the Teflon surface.

∽

Saurav hadn't been able to visit until two months after they moved. Finally, we'll be able to leave, Mala thought when he arrived. She wanted to cry and tell him, 'It's been awful here, it's been awful without you.' But he looked so pale and tired that she had swallowed her list of complaints and served him his dinner. I'll have him to myself afterwards, she thought.

The old lady had talked non-stop through dinner, her voice rising steadily. She bemoaned the disruption of her solitary life, something for which Mala felt a grudging sympathy. But then, she began telling Saurav what was wrong with Mala, telling him that Mala never got the niceties of a superior household, that contrary to what he had proclaimed when he'd decided to marry Mala, class did matter, that the children lacked discipline. Then she told Mala that she had to distance herself from her son, who was just three, or the boy would develop unnatural attachments.

'That's going too far, Mother,' Saurav had interjected.

The old lady shifted in her chair, aggressively thrusting her neck forward, and banged sharply, palm flat, on the table. 'Do you think I am blind, do you think I am lying when I say the children cling to her?' she asked shrilly.

The children stopped playing and moved quickly towards their father, their eyes wide.

'She's their mother. They've been through a lot. Naturally they are close to her when the only other person around ...' His voice was beginning to rise too, but then he looked down at the children and it died with a low gravelly whir. He bent and held them close, mumbling, 'Leave it now, not in front of them.'

'You don't have to protect them from me, I won't ever harm your children!' the old lady had screamed. Saurav had opened his mouth but didn't say anything.

Mala remembered the first time she had heard him speak. It was at a seminar. How she had loved his voice, loved him, loved working alongside him. Why hadn't she stayed on at university, why couldn't she have managed the pregnancies and the research like other women did? She could at least have continued teaching; she was a good teacher. Maybe her job would have survived the cutbacks even when they stopped funding his.

'Okay, enough,' Saurav's mother was saying in a conciliatory tone. 'Tell me about your new job. How many students do you have?' Before he could finish his answer, she'd continued, 'Fourteen-year-olds, that's nice. What is your house like? Do you wear a suit to class – much better than those scruffy research clothes, a suit.'

Saurav had tried to smile in response.

Stop asking him about his job, Mala had wanted to shout. Can't you tell that he hates it, that he wants to go back to his lab? Don't you know that he can't connect to those children, doesn't know what to say to them, that every day is a humiliation?

Her hand had trembled and a spot of sambar plopped on to the white plastic tablecloth with its elaborate pattern of pressed-in flowers and whorls and indents. They all stared at the splash that was thick with the softened lentils. The old lady began to scold as Mala dabbed at the spot, only to spread the yellow of the turmeric powder, the brown of the ground coriander seeds and the red of dried chillies into an ugly stain.

As their grandmother's voice rose, the children disappeared upstairs. Saurav watched them go, then finished his dinner, head bent and shoulders drooping.

Mala wanted to hug him and say, 'It's not your fault, you didn't spill the sambar, I did.' But when they were finally alone, neither of them had wanted to talk about the difficult things they had to deal with. So, she hadn't said anything.

∾

She hadn't seen Saurav for over a month since then. Maybe that's why she was starting to feel sorry for herself. Mala took a deep breath to shake off the paralyzing band of tension and thought, tomorrow she would use her savings and get herself a saucepan. Then, ignoring the old lady, she turned on the stove under the saucepan and dipped the ladle into the vessel of cold milk. As she raised the ladle to pour its contents into the stainless steel pan, the old lady swooped towards her, once again waving the disintegrating non-stick surface at her face.

Mala's back vibrated and cords stood out on her neck. And just like the time when Saurav had visited, her hand shook. A drop of milk splashed on to the counter and another landed on the stove with a hiss. The singed smell of burnt milk entered her nostrils and settled there, an acrid coating over the cloying scent of the old lady's perfume.

Mala returned the ladle to the vessel of cold milk with its dewdrops of condensation and laid her tension-stiff fingers against the chilled curved surface of the metal, watching as she destroyed the evenness of the clean, trembling frost.

'Don't use that pan!' the old lady screeched once more.

And Mala lifted the shiny, stainless steel saucepan, still empty but now red hot, and swung it towards the old lady to ram it into her face. But she smashed it instead on to the granite counter. The metal crumpled and the pan detached from its handle and landed at the old lady's feet.

When the children scampered in for their cocoa, they found their mother on the floor, laughing with her head in her hands. They climbed on top of her and she rolled over on her back, curving her spine to turn herself into a boat for them. One day, soon, I am going to sail away with my children, she thought, as she felt their warm breath on her face.

ABANDONED ROOMS

It is high tide and the view is beautiful. The vileness that washes down from the city is masked by the sparkling water. But my eyes are drawn landward to the dreaded row of insemination chambers that front the yellow edifice of the abandoned Government Breeding Facility. Disintegrating doors hang off their hinges and the insides of the rooms are gaping and empty.

Now that the city's population has climbed back up, the facility has been shifted to new premises, its focus more on research than on production, they say. People come walking here along the seafront now, particularly when it's pretty, like today. But how can they not remember what used to happen here? How can they pretend that the building is a benign entity from another era? Have all traces of the humidity of fertility and breeding vanished from those rooms?

When I was twelve or thirteen, my mother brought

me to see the facility. At that time, the sea wall consisted of crumbling mounds of cement rubble, and the debris that was piled against it – the fermenting, organic waste of unsuccessful breeding experiments – stank of rotting flesh. The noise from the still-functioning incubation engines made a low, terrifying hum. 'Your birthplace,' my mother had whispered, holding my head in her claw-like hands and pulling it down to hers so I had to bend over awkwardly. I remember the feel of her hand in mine as, in my panic, I reached to hold it. The only time I ever did.

I am labelled a failure because I cannot bear children. But some time ago, my body changed and I have discovered that I am capable of breeding. Since then, all I can think about, somewhere in the inner core of my being, is making a child. It's been a year since I started trying to make a life with any male that the underground breeder groups provide. Sometimes there is success, but it doesn't last.

'It's because there is no love,' says my sister Kala as if she, poor unambiguous failure that she is, is an expert. To be fair to her, though, one of the tenets that has been drilled into us is that the basis of love, the very reason we are capable of feeling love at all, is to maintain the species. The rule is, if you can't breed, you no longer have the ability for love. But I have always had a full and dear love for Ka, as rich then as it is now that my hormones are flowing.

I am waiting for her. She and I will join the protest march of failures today. The demonstration is to ask the city to obliterate the breeding facility, our rage with how we are treated focused on the abandoned building.

'Sheena, Sheena,' I hear my sister call. She looks ghastly, poor thing, her hair sparse, the muscles on her face stretched into a sort of permanent grimace. Her eyes are shining, though, and her face struggles into a grin. 'Are we the first? I ran from the station. I knew you'd be early.' She flaps her arms about and her purple-pink sleeves look like fine insect wings. I get up and hug her.

The people enjoying the seafront live a privileged existence in controlled communities behind the walls. They've never seen us rejects, except through the windows of their vehicles when they cross to other suburbs. At the traffic lights, their children stare at us, their eyes so wide, they look like those pictures of lemurs I saw in the Earth's Natural Life Museum that we were taken to from school. I thought then – it was before I went through my development programme so I hadn't yet been told what I was good at, or rather, what I wasn't good at – that it would be fun to try and draw those creatures. I still love to draw even though they've told me I don't have an aptitude for it. After they evaluated me, they placed me in office work; it's dull but much better than the other dreadful tasks I could have been assigned to, such as cleaning excrement or dismembering the dead. Or, worst of all, planting the seeds. I couldn't live with the pain and the screaming and the knowledge that many of the facility's carriers are too young or too old or not developed properly for the task and most of the embryos will die. It is no surprise that so many failures break away from the system.

Despite everything, I haven't broken away from the system. I did think about it once and went to Ka's place to talk to her about it. She lives in one of the illegal colonies. The shacks spring up everywhere – on the edge of the sea, behind apartment blocks, on the hillside – like mushrooms, clinging and pushing, fragile yet densely packed, their dark crevices filled with damp growth. Ka's room overlooks the bridges and hangs off the side of the cliff. The whole area smells of urine. She said I could share her space with her until I found my own residence.

In the end, I compromised freedom for cleanliness and an office routine. It gives me time – time to prepare myself to carry a life.

It was two years ago that I first spotted. The drop on the grey-white bathroom floor was red and round with a trellis of splash marks. When I had gone to see my mother soon after it happened, she'd clutched my tunic, pulled me towards her and said, 'You can breed, I smell your blood. Don't believe what they tell you,

you can breed.' Her breath was foul and she looked like a charcoal drawing, black and powdery, full of shadows and lines. I'd concentrated on extricating my tunic from her fingers. It was the last time I saw her.

I learnt from Ka that I am not the only one showing signs of being fertile. We are mostly female, about the same age, most of us products of this breeding facility. For some reason they didn't scissor the organs out of us but wanted, apparently, to keep us under control with hormones and toxins. Nobody knows why we weren't incarcerated like the caged breeders who are maintained in case the latest engineered beings, with their genes for emotional balance and disease resistance, fail to reproduce. Either we were part of a test group, or somebody decided to spare us. Or perhaps they simply thought they'd successfully suppressed our reproductive systems and transformed us into failures. But our bodies have rebelled and want a part in the creation of life.

I came here today to support my sister in the protest. But I have changed my mind. I wish they hadn't closed the facility down, and I hope it won't be destroyed today. I hope it will be revived. Because I want to have a chance to conceive in a place like this. I'd had no option but to try the illegal insemination shop in the shanties, so dark and dirty. Has it been successful, has it taken? It is too early to say, but it is possible I carry a life inside me.

I move away from the group that disappears into the facility. I dust the grit off the wall and sit down. Young families glance at me as they stroll by, mothers hold their children close. They think I don't fit; can't they see that I too may well be carrying life inside me?

I stop a woman a little older than myself, and point at the building. I want to ask her – what do I want to ask her? I just want to make contact, and have her acknowledge that the building exists and that I exist.

She makes a pretence of looking over at the facility, but I see that she closes her eyes as she turns, as if to shut out the image. She presses her palm on her abdomen – her fingers are short and the veins on the back of her hand are prominent – shakes her head at me and scurries on, bent over, as if our brief encounter has aged her. A child runs up, calling, and reaches for her hand. I see the woman begin to relax. As she and the child walk towards a man selling balloons, her step visibly lightens. I feel as if I can see through to the front of her face and that she is smiling.

I too place my palm on my abdomen, seeking the denseness that could be growing within. I too feel like smiling. The sea is retreating now, revealing the horror that has accumulated underneath. I don't look. I want to keep my mind clear and fill myself with love.

LENNARD-JONES POTENTIALS

'Kanaka, she's the odd one out.' Ma was on the phone and, even though her tone was low in the quiet of the early morning, Kanaka could tell she had gone from being loving to annoyed. 'Hard to believe they are twins, they are so different. Renuka is organized, she has my sense of structure. Even when she's cheeky, she's easy to work with. She's like me.' She paused, listening, then responded with the little laugh she reserved for Pa. 'Oh, alright, Ramu, looks like me too.' Then, her complain-to-Pa voice rose a notch as she said, 'But Kanaka, every morning, every homework session, each meal, it's as if she's in a dream. Sometimes I wonder what part of me is in her.'

Was it only an hour after overhearing that conversation that the water ran out in the bathroom? Foam stung Kanaka's eyes and her feet slid about as she reached for the reserve bucket in the far corner. 'Why can't we keep it closer to the bath area?' Renuka wailed every other day. 'Because I know you girls. If you can reach it easily, you'll just use up the extra water and not refill it for the next emergency,' their mother would reply. Well, apparently Renuka had done just that. The bucket was empty.

Kanaka opened the door a crack. 'Ma!' she bellowed. The thin Kerala cotton towel did little to protect her modesty but she tucked it more firmly around herself and pushed the door a little more. 'Ma, Renu, need water, can you bring me some?'

There was no response and Kanaka remembered they had both left already; Renuka's track training started early this morning and Ma had decided to head straight to the lab after dropping her off at school. When she'd woken Kanaka and told her the morning's plans, Ma had shaken her head and rolled her eyes and added, with a wicked look, 'Now that I am leaving early, I too can be back in time for the cricket.' Ma hated cricket and the fact that almost everyone they knew avidly followed the game and talked about nothing else when the match was on. But just as Kanaka was feeling happy at being included in the grown-up moment of irony, Ma had chided, 'Please make sure, this once, that you're not late for the bus.'

Ma's statement had annoyed Kanaka so much that she had dashed out of bed and into the bathroom, slamming the door shut without saying goodbye. She felt angry enough to want to splash water on the stack of fresh, dry towels. But even as she'd turned on the tap, the stories had begun in her head and her rage had dissipated. She poured mug after mug of water gently over herself, and it ran down the crevices of her body, cool and cleansing, and she felt light and relieved. She began to chat with a man on a cloud, telling him how her ladder twisted into a helix when she tried to reach him. It was a nice conversation; he listened to her and nodded when she told him how some rungs were three-slatted and stronger than others.

The tension of the morning was gone. She tried for a moment to revive it when she opened the door, hair full of shampoo, and called out for more water – just to feel the power and satisfaction of being rude – but the resentment wasn't there any more. Besides which, she realized, there was no one around to direct the resentment at, anyway.

Was she really alone in the house? Kanaka wiped her eyes with the corner of her damp towel and stepped out into the corridor. Every footstep was another adventure; it was impossible to predict where the drops leaving her toes would land. Her heels, however, made distinct pear-shaped marks on the floor, as if they were shallow energy wells rooting her temporarily to the ground. Ma had shown her pictures – contour maps of energy wells. Lennard-Jones potentials, she had called them; that's how lizards attach to surfaces, through really weak bonds, minute attractions between molecules.

I am weakly bonded to the earth, Kanaka thought. She squatted and looked at the water droplets on the floor. The drop that had splashed off her big toe had made a further series of smaller pear shapes. Were they made by the ghosts of my dead sisters who Ma said had died before Renuka and I were born? Kanaka imagined them floating in a petri dish in liquid from their mother's stomach, feeble and small next to Renuka and herself.

Ma said, if they had all been allowed to survive, they would have been seven sisters in all.

Maybe one of them would have been like me, Kanaka thought. What would they have been named; would they all have had names that ended in 'ka' – like Janaka, for example? But Janaka, that's a man's name – Sita's foster father. Pa is our foster father.

She and Renuka didn't know who their real father was, only that it wasn't Pa, and that whoever it was had given his DNA to Ma, to make them. Ma had told them that. Sometimes Kanaka would imitate Pa because he was so lovely and she wanted to be just like him and not like some unknown man she'd never seen. She felt as if she were one of the threads of the twisty molecule that Ma had shown them a model of, saying, 'DNA, it makes us what we are.' Whenever Pa came home from the field, she thought of ways to wind herself a little more around the Pa strand.

Maybe Menaka would have been a good name for

one of her dead sisters, after one of the apsaras. She would have to be the prettiest of the seven. Renuka was the prettier of the two of them and would hate it if one of their dead sisters were prettier than she was. What a fuss she'd made when Kanaka wore Ma's coral necklace at Diwali. There was no point arguing, 'But you wore it last time!' Nor did it make a difference when Ma reasoned with her, saying, 'We agreed you'd let Kanaka wear it on the next occasion.' Soon after that, Ma had split the necklace into two smaller ones. They didn't fight about it any more, but Kanaka always felt sad when she put it on now. And she could tell that Ma did too; it had been *her* mother's.

The marks on the floor were fading, the water evaporating into the air. That's what must have happened to her sisters; they must have pushed higher and higher up the wall of the widening energy well and drifted further and further outwards until they could neither hold on to Ma nor to each other, and simply disappeared.

Kanaka went into the kitchen. The phone was ringing but she didn't answer it. She warmed up the water in the kettle and poured it into a shallow dish. Her head was starting to feel cold, her hair sticky. She bent over the sink. Luckily Ma had put the drain cover on so she didn't have to look down the hole and imagine all the things growing inside. Lifting the cover slightly so as not to block the flow, she scooped up some water in a steel tumbler and used it to pour small quantities over her head. She could feel its warmth as it trickled down her neck and front, dampening the towel even more.

Her chest began to feel cool from all the moisture, so she undid the fabric and swept it around her head to catch all the trickles. Ma's seersucker bathrobe hung on the back of her chair, crumpled and powdery smelling. She wrapped herself in it, and as she did so, she remembered what Ma had said about lizards when she had asked, 'But how do they walk if they are stuck to the wall? How do they lift their feet? Don't they need to be heated or dissolved to let go?'

When you tried to dissolve gummy bears in a glass of water, they got sort of swollen and gooey. Maybe that's what lizards did, even though they weren't in water – maybe they unstuck themselves by getting kind of wobbly. But gummy bears always got a lot harder, less flexible when they dried out and lizards didn't seem to; or maybe they did inside and that's how they got older, like Ma, who always said she was more wobbly but less flexible than her girls.

To Kanaka's question about how lizards detached themselves from the wall, Ma had responded, 'Heated or dissolved! Do you realize you are asking me how they get the energy needed to get out of the well?' and hugged her. Kanaka didn't know why, except that it felt nice.

Then Ma had said, 'That's a great question, Kanaka,' which usually meant she wasn't going to answer. Like when Kanaka had asked how they got the other man's DNA inside Ma's tummy and Renuka had snickered and whispered, 'You can't ask Ma things like that. God, you're such an idiot, don't you know anything,' and Ma had told her it was a good question and asked her to drink her milk and hurry up with her homework.

But about the lizards, Ma said, 'I believe you have something of my mind after all. You're right. They do need a boost, and the lizard brains send a signal to the soles of their feet to say lift up, just as we do. Except, in their case, the molecules on their soles turn around a little and the attraction to the surface to which they are attached is reduced, so they can lift one part up. At the same time, they put another part down and attach, so they don't fall off the wall. Attract, release, attract, release.' She'd laughed and added, 'Sometimes those soft bonds are the wisest.'

Kanaka wasn't really sure what Ma meant by that. But she thought about her family, her father, and Pa and Ma, Renuka and her lost sisters, and she thought she understood. Sometimes you had to be like a soft bond, release yourself, climb out of the energy well so that you didn't crowd it. Lizards lifted one part of their foot up to make room for another. People probably had to let go of one person before they could connect with another. Maybe that's why her father had disappeared, and her sisters, so as to make room. Was it Ma who had given her sisters the boost to go? Had she lifted them so far out that they couldn't find their way back? But how had she chosen which of them would go and which ones would stay? Maybe she hadn't, maybe Renuka and she had simply held on tighter?

Renuka would hold tighter than Kanaka if Ma ever chose between them; Renuka was the one who always won at tug-of-war. Maybe, Kanaka thought, she should make the choice herself rather than wait for the tug-of-war. She could choose to go now, when the house was empty – rise up, and like water vapour, float away. If she breathed in and didn't breathe out, her body would fill with air and she would be buoyant, like a balloon, and catch the currents. Would she drift to where her sisters were? Before pinching her nostrils shut, she burrowed into the dressing gown, covering herself entirely to fill herself with Ma's powdery smell.

When she opened her eyes, Kanaka found herself bundled in the dressing gown and on the kitchen floor, but her head lay cradled in her mother's lap. She was still softly bonded after all.

WE READ THE NEWS

Messages poured in from around the world: we read the news, how are you, we are so concerned, we send our love, know that we care, we hope you were not affected ... Keva could make no sense of them.

In the past, Keva and Samir had also sent messages to friends in disaster zones – friends who had been through war, terrorist attacks, floods, and more. Why didn't her friends in disaster zones ever tell her that the messages made no sense?

She only knew that she had turned into a friend in a disaster zone to someone now.

Andreas called from Zurich. He talked to her for a long time, expressing concern. He also tried to reach her with his professional understanding of trauma. She didn't hear a word. Her neurons had shut down. She functioned using remembered responses. 'Hello' in response to a greeting, then a 'very well, thank you' to the words that were uttered next – words whose meaning she didn't understand.

What occupied her most of the time was the smell – an odour that had settled on her nasal membranes as if they had an independent memory. She knew that the smell emanated from a strange seepage, akin to what flowed through the shallow sewers of a slaughterhouse. The flow had congealed in a crust on her skin, thick and dark brown, like a dried layer of blood and excreta. Fragments of pink fluorescence stuck out of it.

⁊

'It's a beautiful sari, Lakshmi,' Keva had said. She meant it. It was a sharp, rich pink, fluorescent in its intensity, made from the finest, most translucent silk organza. Lakshmi barely acknowledged the compliment. She had nothing nice to say about Keva's clothes either.

Keva had lost weight. It had been hard work, but she had. Her outfit was elegant – a designer one. Sabyasachi. She looked good. But Lakshmi didn't care to notice. Ignoring Keva, she turned to chat with a handsome man whom Keva did not know, while they all waited to be seated.

Samir hadn't yet arrived, and Keva stood on the periphery. She looked around. The structured, architectural floral arrangement – lobster-claw stems extending to the ground from a tall glass tube – made extraordinary shadows on the polished granite wall. The silhouettes of the distinct dark shapes merged with their own gleaming reflections. Keva felt dwarfed – by the flowers, by the shadows, by Lakshmi's lack of interest in her.

Then Samir walked into the restaurant and Keva's spirits lifted. He still did that to her, after all the years together, just the sight of him. She wanted to tell him that, but she could not get to him. She was hemmed in by Lakshmi and the others, and by the granite block on which the flowers stood. Keva watched him, compelling him to look at her.

But when Samir saw Lakshmi, he stopped scanning the cluster of waiting guests. A hint of a smile appeared on his face, an expression Keva thought he reserved only for her. He bent to greet Lakshmi.

Keva had never felt jealous before. She was the centre of Samir's world. She knew that. He made her feel he loved her.

But Lakshmi … For the first time, Keva saw his lust directed at someone other than herself. Lakshmi's dark, narrow waist shone through the pink translucence. He was excited by it, Keva could tell. Lakshmi's hair flicked against his shoulder, she held herself back and Samir leaned into her, breathing in, inhaling her perfume. He kissed her cheek.

He looked up and noticed Keva. He hadn't known she was watching him. A fine, tight fold appeared between his brows. She tried to step forward but there was no way to press through. Then he began to move towards her and people stepped aside for him.

Keva smiled, trying to engage him. Tension lines creased his face and he did not respond. Was he annoyed with her?

'Sorry, sorry,' she mumbled, angry with herself as she put her hand on his arm.

He began to say something to her. What was it? She waited. But Lakshmi interrupted him with 'Samir, about that email I sent you ...' Samir straightened, looking over Keva, and raised his eyelids as if to let in every aspect of Lakshmi's image, eyes transfixed.

Then, suddenly, Samir was throwing himself on Keva. He was heavy. Her elbow jarred into the hard floor. She could hear a shattering staccato sound. A sharp acridity burnt her nostrils. Lakshmi was crashing backwards into her, screaming. Bits of meat flew everywhere. It was not meat from the buffet, Keva registered. They were bits of flesh.

A man lay on top of Lakshmi's legs and her head was flung back. A gory, shredded hole opened in her shining waist – moving, pulsing.

Keva didn't question the new reality. She understood everything and nothing. Her face was sideways on the cool stone floor. Fluorescent fabric covered her. There was a weight on her. Warm weight. Crushing her. She knew not to move.

Her eyes were open, irises expanded in the dim restaurant lighting. Everything filtered through the pink organza. Wide-angle reflections cast themselves directly onto her retina, stimulating her optic nerves bizarrely. The veins of red in the stone floor, natural striations that had been etched centuries ago into the soft limestone strata by rivers of iron, lifted away from the surface. The fine network was alive and dynamic, joining moving – clotted pathways of fluid carmine blood.

She moved her pupils. Carved red lobster-claw bracts were scattered over the beautiful shining ice that covered the floor. A boot crunched on the ice. The pressure didn't crush the crystals, neither did the crystals generate pools of water. It wasn't ice but glass – shards of glass from the vase.

The boot crunched again and a face appeared, young and boyish, with a wild, elevated expression. He was looking down at everyone, peering into their eyes, searching for life. Keva brought her eyelids down, shut out the light, shut out the boy. There was a shout and she heard him withdraw hurriedly. It was safe to look again.

The waiter, Khushrau, was getting up slowly.

Keva never knew one could see so much with one eye. One-and-a-half eyes, for she could see from the eye close to the floor, although her vision was impeded by the bridge of her own nose.

Khushrau stood up. He was tall and gangly and young. He swayed a little, confused, then turned to the dessert buffet that lay in disarray. His fingers looked pale and bony. He straightened the cake stand, dusting off crumbs and arranging the pink and yellow frosted pastries with care.

'Look at that one. He's not dead, the bastard.' And just like in the movies, Khushrau's body began to spray blood and tissue as it lifted and danced to the beat and sound of a gun firing.

Keva's muscles tightened as a scream rose through her chest. But before her throat expanded and her mouth opened, a hand clamped down across her face and Samir's voice said, 'Shh!' Then she heard him say, although there was no sound, 'I love you.'

∽

Keva was at home. She was clean, except for the brown crust of blood and excreta that adhered to her skin. She had washed it with burning hot water and scrubbed it with a pumice stone, but it was still there. She could feel it. She could smell it.

The house was full of people. She could hear her sister talking on her mobile phone in the kitchen. She was describing how the gunmen had entered the restaurant and opened fire. How Keva had been saved by Samir. 'We think he was facing the door and saw the attackers enter – that's what one of the waiters said. He says Samir pushed Keva down. She was lucky, because the granite flower-stand, you know the one at the restaurant entrance, it acted as a shield. There were millions of shards from a broken vase all around Keva, surrounding her, but she didn't have a single cut on her.' Then she lowered her voice and said, 'Her friend Lakshmi was killed.'

Was she my friend, Keva thought.

'They brought Keva home three days ago,' her sister's voice continued. 'She lay under Lakshmi for sixty hours, can you imagine!' Her sister was crying. Her voice was softer but still audible. 'No, no, they haven't found Samir yet.'

He was there, he was there, he was right there, on top of me, Keva wanted to cry out, but she had said so many times and they hadn't heard her.

Her sister was saying, 'We told them that Keva said he was on top of her. But some of the bodies were dragged into a different room. They think Samir's body was taken too.'

But he was alive, Keva was thinking. He covered my mouth and said, 'Shh.'

'Keva insists he was alive, that they couldn't have dragged him away. We've asked them to look. They haven't yet identified the bodies, but they haven't found anyone else alive.'

But he was alive, Keva said in her head. He told me he loved me.

'Yes,' her sister was continuing. 'But I don't know what identification to give them. The problem is, Keva is the only one who knew what he was wearing at the restaurant, and I can't ask her.'

Earlier, when he called, Andreas had said to her, 'I'll explain what you can expect, Keva, so you are not surprised by it.' He told her how for three days she would feel numb, then in one week she would feel terror, and after that her brain would attempt to express the anxieties via nightmares, fear attacks, diarrhoea, chills, rage, panic. The list of reactions was long and meaningless. 'Very well, thank you,' Keva had responded.

'You will see things in your mind that will seem present. Things you remember. Things that you can't possibly remember, that are unreal. They are ways for your brain to block pain and escape the trauma. You will see things your brain wishes to see. Don't worry, Keva, these are normal responses to an abnormal event.'

She'd nodded but he didn't know that.

'Do you hear me, Keva?' he'd repeated. His voice was urgent. 'Physical contact will help you. Hug someone, Keva. Hold someone.'

But Samir wasn't here. How would she hug him?

'Pay attention to me, Keva. I will send you a list of how to cope. Yoga, exercise, healthy food, no coffee ...'

Where was Samir? Did he love her? He told her he did.

❧

Keva stood in the hallway. The doorbell rang. Keva stood still. Someone hurried over from the kitchen and opened the door.

Samir walked in. He was dirty, covered in ash and a brown crust, a soiled bandage around his arm. He smiled directly at Keva.

Keva's entire being exploded with emotion as she opened her arms.

THE PERFECT SHOT

'Ram, you made it home before I did. How fantastic!' Jeeja tossed her sari on the bed and turned the ceiling fan up to maximum, setting up a fierce breeze. The translucent, grey-green fabric that had landed in a pyramid rose and fell with an urgent vibration, and the red silk peacocks of the border fluttered wildly. She lifted her bare arms and said, 'You can't believe what today was like. That stupid Shiromani is pregnant and doesn't fit in any of the clothes any more.' And as she spoke, she twirled and her ankle-length sari petticoat rode up gently.

Ram bent forward, his eyes eager. She smiled at him but continued speaking. 'Oh, I had such a blast at the shoot. We are working on the "Unity in Diversity" series again, and I had to wear a Naga costume. I thought the director's jaw would drop off when I agreed to do it topless. He didn't realize I was going to cover myself with a giant woollen shawl – nothing shows through that.' Then, as Ram reached for her, she laughed, saying, 'Give me a moment to cool down,' and went into the bathroom, leaving the door open..

Her shadow played on the pale, tiled wall as she washed, swiftly bending and straightening, and sluicing mugs of water from a bucket on her feet and arms. When she emerged, the edge of her petticoat was faintly damp and her hair curled around her face.

'Do you know, they are saying the director may lose his job unless he signs some silly paper for the new ministry. But he refuses to do it. Such a bore. Don't know why he can't make a bit of an effort. Even if he doesn't care about us, he could think of the project, at least. If he leaves, they'll probably get some mofussil creep with no taste to do the shoots.'

Ram caught her, his hands on the bare skin at her midriff, and said, 'You shouldn't be doing those pictures for the government, anyway. You need an artist, Jeej – they don't know how to make your beauty come alive.'

'And you do?' She could smell the soap on him, fresh and clean, smell his hair – she was that close – but she didn't touch him.

'Of course I do. I see you, Jeeja. You know that, don't you?'

She nodded and, as she leaned into him, she whispered, 'Yes. I know that.'

∞

'Ram, darling, I can't keep standing here in this transparent thing.' Jeeja took care to hold her pose even as she protested. 'It's chilly. And Maro will be here soon. If she sees me like this, she may end up leaving, like that girl before her who told the whole neighbourhood you photograph me naked.' She launched into a vivid account of the previous maid's stories.

Suddenly he stepped back from the camera, knocking over an easel.

'Ram, I'm sorry, it's nonsense. Nobody pays attention to that rubbish, don't let it ... did I distract you, did I move?'

He staggered and sat down abruptly between the spare stands for the lights, which teetered wildly and crashed.

Jeeja remained frozen for a second, one hand above her head, the other on her hip just as he'd positioned them, before breaking her pose and rushing across to him. 'What's the matter? Shall I call the doctor?'

'Jeeja, I got the letter yesterday, from the ministry.'

'Oh no, not *the* letter. Why didn't you tell me straight away?'

'Yes, the fascist bastards! They say all my work belongs to them. Every shot I ever took.'

'What? Even the ones of me?' He groaned. 'But they don't know you've taken those, do they, Ram? How would they know?' When he didn't answer, she said, 'Those pictures will ruin me, *ruin* me. They'll accuse me of indecency! Damn right-wingers – they don't recognize art unless it looks like a Ravi Varma Lakshmi wrapped in a thick chaddar.'

'They are going to destroy my work, Jeej. Not just the shots of you. The theatre pictures, the buildings, everything. Once I sign my work over to them, they'll destroy it all. That's what they did to Hamid bhai's work – got the rights to it, and then built a big bonfire in front of his eyes. Gelatin silver flames!'

'My god, Ram, what are we going to do? We'll have to hide the prints of me. We can put them between my saris and take them to my grandmother's. Just give them the other stuff, the stupid wedding work and things.'

'Impossible, Jeeja, impossible!' He clutched himself, holding his wiry frame tight, and rocked back and forth. 'There's no time to hide anything. They want my decision today.' His face was contorted as he said, 'I won't give in to them. They can't survive in power forever. I didn't want to tell you because it doesn't make a difference to our work. I won't have any of it halted. I won't let them destroy anything. I'll simply not sign.'

Jeeja shivered and stood up. She straightened the aluminium stands, dusted herself off, picked up a paisley shawl that lay on a chair and wrapped it around her shoulders. 'You'll lose your job if you don't sign. You know that, don't you?'

When he didn't reply, she moved to the wall and touched the prints he had taped there. They were ones he had taken of her over the past week, some in the studio, some in the garden, one on the bed. In each one, he'd wanted her to look directly into the camera, as if he was trying to look through her eyes to what was inside her. The 'source of her beauty', he called it. He was so obsessed with the idea, and yet she had no sense of what it was he sought, or if it even existed. She wondered if he would ever stop believing he could find it.

He raised his head and watched her. Then he cried out, 'Without photographing you, I am nothing, I can't understand light and shade if I can't shoot you. I can't jeopardise that. I can't sign.'

She couldn't bear to look at him as she said, 'I'll have to stay with the government job. You know that, don't you, Ram?'

'No, no! You can't do that.'

'We can't survive otherwise. What other jobs are there? Besides, I can't give up my career for your principles. The ministry photographers love me; they want to use me for all the publicity.'

There was silence. Then he said with a sob, 'No, Jeeja, no. I couldn't bear it, thinking of you there. Give it up, we'll find a way. We'll be together – no prize-giving ceremonies, no foreign visitors, no tourism work – just us.'

She walked out of the studio and could hear him calling out, 'We'll concentrate on the art, really concentrate. We'll get the perfect shot.'

∽

'A little to the right,' he said. 'Tilt. That way. What aren't you understanding? The light, I want the light on your cheekbone, goddamn it.' Ram put his head to the eyepiece, bending carefully, his body not touching the meticulously set up tripod. But as he tightened for the shot, like a cat coiling to spring, a faint breeze blew in from the window and the curtain fluttered, causing a shadow to ripple across her face. 'Fuck!' he shouted. 'Sultana! Get here. Now!'

Jeeja wished Ram wouldn't call Maro that. He called out again, his voice pitched higher. The skin on Jeeja's cheek began to pucker faintly in the chill. She hoped that Maro would hurry. He had become so obsessive about the shots of her now that if her skin didn't look right to him, he would be upset. The other photographers she worked with were much less particular. Her face was everywhere these days – in magazines, on billboards. If the ministry had found those compromising pictures of her, her career would have been over. Even though it had ruined Ram, she was relieved that he hadn't signed away the rights of his works – the moral police would have crushed her. It made her feel terribly guilty, though, all his publishing permits taken away, watching him humiliated and rejected and falling apart. It stopped her from protesting as he got more and more irritable and aggressive.

'What the hell, Sultana. What took you so long? Your

husband bedding you on a Saturday morning?' Luckily he spoke in English and Maro didn't understand him, or so it seemed. Jeeja didn't dare move her head but indicated the curtains with her eyes. Maro wiped her hands swiftly on her pallu and, with a grimace that emphasized the dark shrivelled aspect that had inspired Ram's nickname for her, hurried to the window. There, she crouched, making sure that she and her shadow stayed out of the light as she held the curtains back.

'At least the old raisin has learnt something,' Ram muttered and focused on the image once again. His finger was bent, taut above the button. He pressed and there was a swift series of mechanical clicks before he raised his head. Jeeja breathed, releasing the tension, but held her pose. This was just the first shot. Only when he moved away from the camera did they all relax.

Immediately, Jeeja tugged her sari petticoat from low on her hips back up to her waist and covered her upper body with the end of her sari. It destroyed the soft, pre-Raphaelite drapery she'd affected for the shot. It had taken her and Ram a full half hour to arrange, his perfectionist eye ensuring that the pleats were proportioned just right while she held them at her shoulder, gently, so the fluidity of the material about her waist and hips wasn't stretched or perturbed. He'd asked her to wear crêpe silk and chosen the colour, even though he was shooting in black and white. 'The density of the primary hues is so different from pastels,' he'd said, when she had first become his muse. Nowadays he rarely spoke about the craft to her.

When all the pleats were in position, he'd used one of the super large paperclips he'd saved from a more hopeful time in America, fastening the material to the blouse, behind her shoulder. She usually knew what kind of posture he expected her to adopt from how he dressed her for the shot. But she always waited for him to tell her how to pose. Sometimes he surprised her. But even when he didn't, even when she'd predicted every twist and tilt he wanted, even in the days when he wasn't on the edge of losing it all the time, it put him in a bad mood if she didn't allow him to direct her. 'Turn a little, twist from the waist, look over your left shoulder, right shoulder back and up.' The instructions seemed to prepare him for the shot.

When Ram left the room, Jeeja stepped down from the pedestal. 'Maro, can you pick up the baby? I'll change my sari first,' she called as she hurried out of the door. The baby had stopped whimpering a while earlier. He seemed to have realized that yelling only made his mother take longer to give him her attention.

In the bedroom, she looked at her waist in the mirror. It was not as it used to be when it first caught Ram's eye, but it was still slim. 'I hope that won't happen to you,' he'd said once when his sister had sent them a photograph of her new baby. The snapshot was ill composed, including little of his sister's doting face and a substantial view of the loose, post-partum spread of her belly. 'She's happy,' Jeeja had replied smugly and they'd both smirked.

She'd made sure her waist was still a seductive part of her even after the baby, asking Maro to fling alternate mugs of ice-cold and burning hot water on her abdomen starting just weeks after the birth. She pulled the cotton sari tighter so her curves weren't obscured, and smoothed the folds over herself. She smiled ruefully – even though he was horrid and self-destructive these days, she still wanted his attention and revelled in the idea that he was searching for her soul, that she was still his true muse.

She took out her box of kajal. Ram didn't like her wearing too much for the shots. It spread in the heat of the lamps, he said. But she was generous now as she leaned into the mirror.

He was at the dining table, frowning at a print, as she went to the kitchen to get the baby. Since the shoot had gone well, he would be calm, she thought, and bent to touch his shoulder. Ram looked up. His gaze rested on her darkened lids, then moved down her body, but swung back up and locked on her eyes. He frowned, and his expression changed before he returned to the print.

'He sees me again, don't you think?' she whispered to the baby who gurgled back. She looked in the mirror on the kitchen door and examined herself. 'I thought for a moment that he was annoyed, that I had worn too much kajal, that it had smeared. But it isn't that, he is beginning to get his eye back, I think.' Maro, to whom this last was addressed, was chopping beans fiercely and didn't answer. 'Yes, that's it,' Jeeja mumbled, 'he sees me again.'

When Ram disappeared into his studio, she tried to follow him. Sometimes, if she rubbed his back, tired from bending over the light box, he relaxed and shared things with her again.

He was on the phone and glared at her when she entered. 'Yes, the morning shoot,' he was saying. He was speaking to that girl, she realized.

Jeeja wished she had never brought the girl into the studio. But she had been so tired after the baby and he had been so persistent, so finicky about detail, complaining of the tiredness of her skin, the shadows under her eyes, her lack of enthusiasm. 'Please, Ram, not another early morning shot?' she'd finally had to plead. And even though he complied, he was angry. She found the girl, an out-of-work model, through her contacts at the agency. She seemed to please him. Even when Jeeja had been ready to pose for him again, Ram had suggested that the girl continue. 'She has good lines, very good lines,' he'd said, 'and she's willing.'

Willing? Willing to do what? Why had she permitted it? Jeeja's stomach burnt.

'The shot has to be in the first light of morning,' he used to say to her. That's how he'd wooed *her* all those years ago, seducing her into staying in the studio and waking her with gifts that transported her into smiling straight at him when she posed. The only time he woke her up early these days was to make tea for the girl. When she asked him about it, he was dismissive, saying, 'She is nothing, Jeeja, just an empty body' – a statement that had disturbed her all the more.

∽

'Beauty!' His voice was high, shrieking. 'I'm not afraid of beauty.'[*]

Signalling to Maro that she take the baby for a walk, Jeeja opened the studio door. She hadn't stepped inside for weeks. The normally light-filled room was dim, the curtains drawn shut. Ram lay splayed on a large pile of torn prints scattered on the floor. She turned on a table lamp. A photograph of herself in the paisley shawl, the folds pulled tight over her pregnant stomach, lay crumpled under his right foot.

'Fucking useless stuff,' he said. 'A lifetime of it.'

'But I love that picture, Ram,' she said softly, picking up the fragment.

'You love it,' he mimicked. 'Do you think he does too?' He waved a crumpled newspaper at her face. 'Every day, I've shot you. Every day. Who is this

---

[*] 'I'm not afraid of beauty' – quoted from a statement made by Anish Kapoor during a discussion with Homi Bhabha, at the National Centre for the Performing Arts, Mumbai, in 2010. Used with permission.

bastard? Do you think he knows how to take your picture?' It was an edition from last week, an article about her. How had Ram got hold of it? He hardly ever left the studio now, let alone the house, and she made sure no magazines or newspapers with pictures of her entered the house.

'Art!' he screamed, banging the paper on the floor. 'The bastard talks about art.'

'It's rubbish, Ram, you know it. He simply creates publicity shots, it's not art.'

'How many layers did you take off for that picture? Huh, tell me that. Exposing yourself! And how come the government allows this? Those puritanical fascists, they stick their noses into my art, they don't write about my work. How come they are allowing this photo? What did you do to make them print it?'

'That's a vile suggestion, Ram, and I resent it. It's a perfectly decent photo. Besides, have you forgotten, it's a different party in power now. These guys are just money-mongers, they don't care about anything, least of all nudity.' She bent, took hold of his shoulders and shook him. 'Get up! What's wrong with you? You were the one who refused to go to work when they were hiring – your principles, you said. And when they asked you to take your old job back, you were the one who said you wouldn't stoop to taking photos of people you didn't respect. Naturally they don't write about you.'

'They write about you.'

'Yes.'

'And they photograph you.'

'Yes.'

Ram sat up and flailed his arms. Bits of photographs flew about. A fragment with Jeeja's eye stuck to his sweat-dampened face, a piece of her extended leg landed on his shirt. He began to sob. 'I see you, Jeeja, you look at me with your kajal-darkened eye, and my insides twist with the intensity of it. But every day I catch it less, every day you give less of yourself to me. Look.' He picked up a picture. It was one he'd taken in the garden in the winter; she could see a bit of the rose bush in bloom. She remembered that it was a few weeks after the baby and she hadn't wanted to do the shoot. He waved it at her. 'Why do you escape me, why? You don't shine at me any more. Where are you? Where are you, Jeeja?'

She knelt and put her arms around him, pulling him gently down to lie beside her. She needed him. She needed him as much as he needed her. And all the governments and censors in the world were not going to change that. She was afraid it might almost be too late for them to recover. Was it an hour afterwards that they moved, or a day, Jeeja couldn't tell. It was Ram who first stirred. 'Come,' he said, and raised her up. He drew back the curtains, letting in the light. 'Stand by the window,' he said. 'No, don't wipe your face. Just like that, as you are. I want to catch you as you are.'

THE SHIFT

The water seemed to shift from grey-brown to slate black with a choppy, circular movement. Kay moved with the waves, recalling the wonder of seaside holidays when she would lose herself in the brilliance that surged underneath.

Today's water drew an opaque veil over the world below. She couldn't even discern Nasir's feet, feet that floated so tender and loyal alongside hers. Perhaps it meant that Nasir wasn't there beside her any more. Had he drifted off? Or maybe, despite everything they'd thought about and discussed, he'd directed himself away from where the waves were taking them. He'd never been able to let go and float as Kay could. She had stamina in the sea, and that was because she could give herself up to the movement, not fight and flail and strain to keep her head above the water as Nasir did. That might have been the reason it came to her first, the idea, the plan, call it what you will.

The first time she took her clothes off for him, he stood before her, still and shy and compelled. She had felt then, and she felt even now, that she could give herself up completely to him. Just as she did to the water when she entered the ocean. 'We are perfectly balanced,' she said to him.

When the memory of her mother's mouth, stretched and ugly, teeth bared in anger, and her father's despairing face as he hopelessly repeated, 'We can repair it,' flashed into her mind, she thought, we must float away, Nasir and I, before it gets spoilt.

Initially, Nasir couldn't accept the notion. 'What? Just give up, let go of life so easily?' But then the possibility that they could drift together into eternity penetrated his sensibility and it was as if it was he who thought of it first. 'That way, Kay, we never have to suffer. We can be happy forever,' he said. He couldn't think of how to do it, though. It was she who suggested they should be in the open – that it should be free, suspended, effortless.

'I am a yogi in the water,' she said to him, 'relaxed, surrendering.' And he said, 'That's beautiful,' adding, 'the sea, that's the right way. We can float to the horizon, side by side.'

∽

'I am pregnant, Nasir.' Kay imagined herself saying it.

In her telling, the first time she imagines it, she and

Nasir are seated at the breakfast table. She can see herself and she can see herself looking at him. The light is shining on her face, on the tea in the glass cups, on the string of jasmine that lies white on the wooden surface. It is shining on the drops in his wet hair, making them glisten. Kay sees the scene that her mind's eye has created. In the image, her lips are forming the words, 'I am pregnant, Nasir.' She can see that. But he has bent forward, and she cannot see his face, cannot see his eyes. She doesn't know how he feels.

The second time she imagines telling him she is pregnant, they are walking through the rain. Above her calves, her body, her spirit respond to the rain and everything is romantic – the soft drizzle, the coolness, the laughter. But below, the street is filled with trash and the water is tainted with infection. She is joyous, yet fearful. In her image, he is turning to her, she is about to see how he feels, when he grabs her elbow to help her avoid a treacherous puddle.

❧

'Come, follow, swim after me,' she said to him as they stepped into the water. 'I'll go real slow past the rocks. After that, we drift. Don't push against the current. Just drift.'

Nasir nodded. His skin puckered faintly with the cold.

Kay laughed. 'Don't think about it and the cold will

go away. One more stroke, Nasir, and you're clear of the rocks. That's it. Just let go now, let go and float.'

'Kay, I am afraid.'

'Remember, Nasir, if we let go and float, we never have to see it go sour.'

'Into eternity together?'

The water seemed to shift, choppy and circular, from grey-brown to slate black as they drifted. And then, Nasir wasn't there beside her any more. Had the current pulled him away or had he chosen to move off? Did it matter? He wasn't there.

Kay thought of the minute being floating inside of her. 'I am pregnant, Nasir,' she said.

'We are complete,' Nasir mouthed through the salt spray. Where had he appeared from? 'We are complete.'

Taking her hand, he began to swim back to the shore, awkward, yet shining with love.

WHEN THE CHILDREN
COME HOME

Poulumi's high-pitched lilting, 'Doll baby, doll baby ...', might have been taken for a religious chant – a thousand descriptives of the goddess, a hundred and eight invocations for good fortune. Every now and then, however, she paused, breaking the rhythm – sometimes as she extricated a bright plastic toy that had got tangled in the strands that hung down from her sweater, sometimes as she stood behind Soumitro and waited for him, shoulders slumped, to speak to her. Only when her fine fingers worked the wool was it evident that her body inside the shambling mass of clothes was small-made and fragile. She laid those fingers now on Soumitro's shoulder and said, 'When Chiro and Apo come home, I'll put the animal quilt on Apo's bed. She loves the camels and the horses and the birds on it. Na, don't you agree, Soumitro?'

Hunched over the computer, Soumitro's body

seemed to turn even more inward upon itself at her question and he stared at the screen without responding. She shuffled off, continuing to mutter a disconnected stream of words while she moved toys from one end of the room to the other. He dragged his chair closer to the desk and drew his blanket tight.

'I am cold. Can we put the heating on, Soumi?' Poulumi was at his shoulder again. Even though her skin shone soft in the light from the terminal, her young lips were chapped and indented where she had bitten down on them.

Making incoherent sounds, she pulled out a black shawl with a delicate embroidered border from under a pile of clothes on the back of his chair. A messy tangle of things collapsed on to the floor. With a sibilant cluck he bent to pick them up but shrank back when he spotted a pair of children's hoodies in the pile. They had fallen with sleeves outstretched, as if reaching out with their scruffy blue and pink crushed velvet arms, grotesque in the bright glow of the desk lamp.

The doorbell rang and Poulumi grabbed the hoodies and held them to her chest. 'Why someone's ringing so late? What's happened, Soumitro?' Her fingers picked at the garments, shedding pastel fluff on the dirty beige carpet. 'Why they are coming after dark?' Her voice rose sharply.

He pulled the blanket over his head and said, 'It's four o'clock only. What, you think this is India, dark means late? It is middle of afternoon, I am working. Open the door.' She shook her head and he repeated, 'Open the door. I am saying, open the door.'

'I can't, Soumitro. Please. You go. They are ringing again and again.'

After the third ring, he rose. His grey sweatshirt rode up, revealing an unwieldy back and a sagging pair of checked boxer shorts. He yanked his sweatpants up and went to the door.

'Oh, hello, hello, Hege. Please to … please to come inside.' Soumitro leaned forward from the waist as he ushered in a tall, fine-haired, dehydrated-looking woman who brought a waft of an artificial fragrance, shampoo or deodorant, into the stale curried air of the room. 'Please, please.' Soumitro indicated the sofa.

'It's Hege, Poulumi. From the town office, you know, the social service lady. Clear the sofa, clear the sofa.'

Poulumi remained where she was, twisting and mangling the hoodies into a pastel velvet rope.

'Sit, sit, please sit.' He picked up a pile of papers from the sofa, shuffled them together in a haphazard way, and put them on the chair. Most of them slid off and landed on the fallen clothes. 'The permission has come for working from the house till situation is cleared. The company has agreed for me to be with my wife at this time. You see.' He picked up an envelope from the table and held it out.

The lady ignored him and said, 'I am here about the

children, Mr Bose.' She looked down at a note in her hand and said carefully, 'Chirodeep and Aporna.'

'Yes, yes, the children. She is here about the children, Poulumi.'

'My children, now they will be returned?' Poulumi asked. 'Where are my children? My Chiro, my Apo, I am waiting, waiting.'

'Your children are safe, Mrs Bose. Please be calm.' Hege perched on the edge of the sofa, her body held tight, as if allowing herself only minimal contact with anything in the room. She took a file out of her briefcase and repeated, 'Your children are safe. I am in charge of them now.'

∽

The leaves of the ficus on the balcony had begun to fall and Apo's hair was turning frizzy in the humidity. The sensation in her fingers as she smoothed it took her back to a time when her hair used to stay soft and silky even when the leaves fell. A time when the fallen foliage was orange and yellow instead of brown or green, like now. A time when leaf fall meant the air was clear and crisp and, instead of the frangipani with its waxy white flowers that glowed ivory in the heat, she had looked up at papery bright blossoms that a tall, fair-haired lady had told her were called petunia. Not wanting to visit those memories, Apo stood still.

Her phone beeped. Relieved, she went quickly

towards the bright blue screen. It was a message from Chiro. C u in hf hr, it said.

She looked at herself in the mirror. The white kurta with the delicate silver kadi print set off her golden-brown skin and eyes. She smoothed her hair down again. Then she went around the apartment, straightening the glass cat on the desk, moving the stems of the flowers so the pink and yellow gerberas alternated, adjusting the precision of alignment of the stacked books on her bedside table. She picked up her silver-grey umbrella from the orange metal bucket near the front door that matched the orange pencil container by the telephone. Then, opening her white door, she headed out.

⚬

'No, no! Are you crazy?' Apo's hand shook and chai spilt into her saucer. She put her cup down and dabbed at the barely visible splatter on her white kurta with a kerchief that she dipped in the glass of water in front of her. 'I am not coming with you to see her.'

They were at a corner table in the cafe that she liked for its neat sandwiches and white tablecloths. Each time she agreed to meet Chiro, she persuaded herself that it was because he wanted to be more amenable, more manageable. This time he will listen to me, she would tell herself. He will clean himself up. This time he will not obsess about our mother and will agree to go to the classes I have enrolled him in. But this time too, like every other time before, he said, 'Ma wants you to come. She's asking and asking.' He scratched his beard and flakes from the samosa he had eaten extended the pattern of dandruff and scuffed skin on his black kurta.

Apo stared, then said, 'God, you came straight from her, didn't you? You went to tell her we were meeting, didn't you?'

Chiro ducked his head and took a sip of his tea. It dripped on to the table and the floor.

'You're disgusting.' Her delicate fingers tightened on the tissue as she wiped her own saucer clean. She leaned towards him and added, 'You stink, Chiro. When was the last time you had a bath? And look at your hair! Where did you sleep last night? You didn't go home, did you? Did you stay at the hospital?'

'Not allowed. You know that. Ma wanted me to stay. But the ward sister made me leave. Ma was crying and crying and asking for you.'

'That's rubbish. Don't tell me that shit. She doesn't know who I am. She never knew even when Nani took me to see her after we were brought back. I was only four, tiny, but I remember. It made Nani cry. I hate that place.'

'Don't talk like that, Apo.'

'Sometimes I think I am the only one in this family who has any sense of order. Look at you. And Mother in that mental hospital. Just a disaster. And Father is worse – left us for years with Nani. Didn't he know that you never went to school, that you ran away and stayed out for months looking for Mother, that you barely know how to read and write? Didn't he care? And now, always drunk and whining about how he was ruined by us. I am the only one who can look after myself. I think the fairies must have dropped me into this family.'

∽

'My beautiful Apo,' Poulumi cooed. She cradled a broken plastic doll in her hands. 'Doll baby, doll baby,' she repeated, swaying from side to side.

Apo stood against the wall, not touching the concrete surface, and glared at Chiro.

'She's happy,' Chiro said.

'Yeah, fuck, I see that.'

'No, it's true. She knows somehow you are here. Most of the time she doesn't hold the doll baby these days.'

After a pause Chiro said, 'You know, Apo, when the lady used to bring us for a visit, you would look like a foreign baby. I would run to Ma, but the lady, she held you all the time, saying, "I'm her mother now, Mrs Bose." When Nani was finally given the papers and came to take us, the lady kept holding you, not giving you to Nani. And, by then, Ma, she didn't know anything any more.'

A dog was barking outside and Poulumi raised her head. 'Dogs are dangerous – they take away babies. I saw it in the TV. People also, they are dangerous. The lady took away my baby. Hege took her.' Poulumi's voice turned high-pitched. '"Stay calm, Mrs Bose. Your children are safe, Mrs Bose." But I took my baby back. I took her from Hege and ran and ran.' She started to walk fast about the room. 'Ran and ran, ran and ran. In the dark, feet turning to ice, I ran and ran.' Beads of sweat stood out on her upper lip and the sheen of perspiration made her arms, bare in a sleeveless housecoat, glow. Suddenly she sat on the floor and held herself between her legs. 'You have to put ice down there, you know. To keep it cold. Ice. Or you make more babies, more small babies. Can't make more babies. They take them away.'

She crossed her splayed legs and patted the floor. 'Come, sit here.' She gesticulated at Apo, who remained where she was.

'They caught me. Took the baby away again. Did you look after her, Chiro?'

'Yes, Ma. I did.'

'Even after they sent me away. Did you look after her?'

'Yes, Ma. And now we are here.'

Poulumi held the doll out to Apo. 'Take it. The baby.'

'If I touch that thing, I'll throw it out to the dogs,' Apo said.

But when Chiro looked at her, she held out her arms, feeling every fibre of muscle elongate in her neck, her shoulders, her arms, her fingers as they reached towards her mother.

DOES THE WORD EVEN EXIST
IN OUR LANGUAGE?

Surya's grandmother and mine were cousins many times removed. No one who can trace the relationship survives, but everyone knew that as girls, fifty or sixty years ago, the two had been inseparable. I happened to be present the very last time they met. It was at a family wedding just before Surya's grandmother died.

'Shailaja, Shailaja,' she'd called out.

I had never heard anyone call my grandmother by her name. Most people called her Ajji, as if she were some universal grandmother with no other role but to be benign. On rare occasions I'd heard her referred to as Usha Bai, the name she'd been given by her husband's family when she was married at thirteen, presumably because they felt the moniker better suited the alignment of the stars that ruled their household. I wonder if it had given my grandmother a happier life.

'Shailaja, Shailaja.' Surya's grandmother's voice had been soft, yet it had carried over all the other noises at the wedding hall.

Ajji hurried forward, her eyes bright with tears. Just then the drums sounded, fast and insistent, accompanied by the sharp, reedy melody of the nadaswaram announcing the tying of the nuptial knot. 'Maalu. My dear Maalu.' Ajji's body bent at the waist as if her whole body was reaching towards her friend. Malathi Bai extended her arm and gently touched Ajji's elbow. They walked slowly together to the folding steel chairs near the fan and sat there, hardly speaking.

'Why didn't you talk more to her, Ajji?' I'd asked when we got home.

'What is there to say, Ramu?' she'd replied. With everything I know now, I could counter – what is not there to say? But at that time, I nodded as if I understood.

Anyway, when Malathi Bai's grandson, Surya, contacted my mother to say he and his fellow students from their university study group had to spend three weeks in an Indian village, there was no question of them not coming to our village, or what was left of it, subsumed as it was by the city.

⚭

The students arrived one morning around eleven, an odd scruffy bunch. In addition to their appearance, their coarse, wide-mouthed tones drew us in and we gathered close to stare as they unloaded their things on our dusty main street.

They were obviously taken aback when they found that the village was not some idyllic pastoral place but an ugly cluster of small concrete structures creeping in from a city that was fast encroaching upon our outskirts. It was only when one looked in the direction of the lake that one found any evidence of the tiled mortar buildings and granite courtyards that had characterized the area.

Some of the students, like Surya, stayed in the village while others were housed in a nearby hostel. They were like alien creatures – the noises they made, their daily routines completely unlike ours. They were skilled at getting their way too, not intimidated about asking for what they wanted, as I imagined I would be if I were to visit their place. One of the girls said with a pout and a hug, 'Oh, the bathwater is cold. Papamma, can't I have hot water, please?' Papamma set to lighting the fire to heat the water.

A few years ago, someone left the fire unattended under one of Papamma's trees and scorched it to death. Every leaf had curled in brown agony and fallen to the ground. Papamma had cried and moved the spot where she lit the fire to one where there was no shade. This was fine most of the time, since the water was only heated in the early mornings or during the cool winters.

But this student rose at noon and only wanted to bathe in the middle of the blazing summer afternoon. And to my surprise, Papamma heated the water, using up mountains of good firewood in the process.

'Thank you,' the girl would simper as the older woman carried in buckets of steaming water, perspiring and red from the effort. Then, bending ineffectually, the girl would add, 'Don't lift it, I can do it,' after it was done. I don't know why Papamma didn't just say, 'Bathe in cold water,' as she would have to her own grandchildren. Maybe the foreignness of the girl was intimidating.

'Why are you here?' I asked one of the students. 'Beats going to class,' he replied. What did that mean?

I got a better answer when I asked Surya. 'Why am I here? Treasure, my boy. Looking for treasure.' He was laughing when he said it, but I knew he was serious. Many people had searched for Tipu Sultan's treasure chest that was supposed to have been buried in the sand near the lakebed. There was a perpetual debate about whether it contained coins or jewels. Some even said it was filled with chopped body parts of Tipu's family.

'Don't worry, Suryanna. You'll see, it will be full of gold, not bones,' I said, wanting to reassure him that our village, our connection, and thus somehow, *I*, wouldn't fail him.

'Gold?' he roared. 'This is bigger than gold. We are looking for real treasure, my boy.'

More valuable than gold? I laughed too, uncomprehending but excited.

Surya had a handsome face and a large unwieldy body. And a friendly charm. He was more disciplined than the rest of the group. He rose early, even when he'd stayed out late with the others. Once he was up, all he seemed to do was wander about and talk to anyone who was around. I was fascinated and tagged along, happy when he paid attention to me, bored when he asked people, again and again, for versions of old tales that none of us cared about.

The only time I enjoyed the stories was when he spent time with my grandmother. He would ask her questions about subjects that none of the family ever broached. Responding to the encouraging sounds he made, my grandmother would forget I was around, forget she had spent a lifetime hiding the family history from me, and talk – about her son, the alcoholic recluse; about my mother, widowed and lonely; and about her own late husband's mistress who lived in the next lane and who, my grandmother said, had given her husband something she never could.

One day I walked into our cool, dark hall with its old rosewood table and chair. In the moments it took for my eyes, obscured by the afternoon glare, to adjust to the dimness, I saw my grandmother wiping her eyes with the edge of her cotton sari. 'I wish,' she was saying, softly. By the time I blinked a few times and could see again, she was sitting in her usual posture, erect and gracious in her chair, her head tilted solicitously towards us.

That evening, Surya whispered excitedly into the phone, 'Bonanza, man! You won't believe what I just learnt.' He looked up as I entered, straightened, and changing his tone, started talking loudly about a walk along the lake bund where there was a crumbling mortar structure. I knew, and I knew that he knew there was nothing there. Why was he deliberately misleading whomever he was talking to?

∽

Generally, the April holidays were a nightmare. I had to resist the activities my mother tried to enrol me in at the high school while she was at work. This time, however, her energies were distracted by a new colleague; so I was left to myself.

While my mother was relieved that I was busy following Surya everywhere, she was irritated too. 'Gone all day again,' she said with a bitterness that had nothing much to do with me – she was bitter about everything in those days. 'Well, I don't care what you do, so long as you don't get into any trouble. And are back on time. Also, make sure you practise. Just because your violin teacher has traipsed off on holiday – imagine, she has gone to Disneyland when you and I can't go anywhere – doesn't mean you don't keep up with practice.'

To appease my mother, I would take out the violin in the hot, torpid afternoons and play wild, wandering versions of tunes I had been taught. Surya would take a siesta or work on his laptop – a sleek, city-looking device that he stored under his bed in a soft velvety-grey, envelope-like case. Occasionally I would drop my bow and try to read over his shoulder as he typed, but he would shoo me away with a laugh, saying, 'No peeking. This is a treasure hunt, remember – every man for himself. We each have to follow our own clues.'

'How can I recognize the clues? I don't know what I am looking for.'

'Man, there's treasure everywhere,' he said, laughing again. 'Just look around. Look around, and listen. Listen!'

⁂

They hadn't found anything. I would have known if they had. But they spent their last week working together and typing furiously on their computers rather than doing any more searching.

They used the house of Mrs Kamala, the widow, for this final stretch. Her place was at the other end of the village, out of bounds for me. My mother distrusted Mrs K's lifestyle. 'Why does she hang around near the gate, waiting to chat with every passer-by?' I heard her saying to my grandmother.

I finally worked up the courage to sneak off to Mrs

K's. She happened to be in the garden, and took my arm and led me in. The small, pink-distempered hall had plush upholstered sofas arranged in a sharp square around a low glass-top table. The students lay about with their computers, their dirty feet everywhere.

'Poor things, they work so hard,' she said as she looked around. 'I have to provide refreshments.' She took out a bottle of ancient whisky from a musty cupboard filled with her dead husband's clothes. 'He was saving it for something special,' she said with a sad smile. Then she perked up, took out some glasses and said, 'Please, please, take some!'

The group drank greedily once they got over the fact that the Scotch had apparently been wrapped in old-fashioned underwear for many years. Surya, who was leaning over his computer as one of the girls read out to him from a notebook, looked up and grinned and winked at me. I felt left out and embarrassed.

That week, my mother arranged for me to take maths classes to prepare for entering high school. And in a few days, the group left.

'They've tossed their cardboard boxes into my storm drain!' Mrs K cried the morning after their departure as I wandered past her place to convince myself they were truly gone. 'I'd had the drain cleared just before they arrived.' Her fingers anxiously balled up the material of her sari as she lifted it with both hands before stepping outside her compound wall.

The border of the grim flowered print played at her skinny calves. 'Cheeky things! When I asked them to clean the verandah before they left, they said, "Yes, Mrs K, no problem, Mrs K." And now look at the pulp that's clogged up everything.' She gesticulated with both hands at the disintegrating boxes in the drain. A fine layer of sweat gathered in the creased pockets below her eyes. She sighed and used the end of her sari to dab at her face, leaving a crushed rosette shape in the fabric she released. 'I wonder why they were here? What did they want from us?'

෴

'The unscrupulous creep! I knew I shouldn't have let him into our lives. Thank god your grandmother is no longer with us.' My mother tossed the book she was holding into the wastepaper basket and dusted off her fingers with a grimace.

My mother had been annoyed when Surya didn't keep in touch, but that was a couple of years ago and she soon gave in, with an odd pleasure, to other, more pressing melancholies involving that colleague who was now her beau. But whatever Surya had now sent made her angrier than I'd seen her in a while. She picked up the bulky yellow envelope with the Abraham Lincoln stamps and extricated a letter. Holding it by the corners, as if it were something dirty, she read out loud. 'Hello, dear friends.'

What the hell did he mean by 'dear friends'? I was the one who'd been his friend. My mother was my mother and my grandmother was dead. I cursed loudly. My mother glanced at me, continued reading quietly, then exclaimed, 'The pompous ass.' She crumpled the letter and threw it so it landed right next to the book.

As soon as I had a chance, I retrieved the book from the wastebasket and took it to my room. Finally I would find out what their stay was about; what they had been searching for.

The introductory essay went on about folk tales and oral histories. No mention of the treasure. There was a section about the psychological implications of covert lesbian affairs on the dynamics of the village. Lesbian? Here? In our village? Did anyone know that word? Did it even exist in our language? Next, there was a bit about extra-marital relationships – men and their mistresses. There was a section on feminism and freedom, and I thought of Papamma and how all those grand concepts hadn't trickled down in their attitude towards her. Abstract theoretical terms – gender hegemony frameworks and so on – ran across the pages.

I laughed. This stuff had nothing to do with our small, conventional, characterless, squeezed-in corner of the city that, through developmental neglect, still retained some aspects of the village. This book was about some other interesting place.

I flipped to the chapter on the lesbian affair, which sounded like a promising read for the afternoon. I was surprised to see that it was written by Surya.

The story began with a description of an elderly lady, separated from her female lover by an unfulfilling marriage. The lady was described in great physical detail, down to her soft pink saris. It was without doubt my grandmother. And her lesbian lover? Malathi Bai, Surya's grandmother! I understood why my mother had flung the book away. It all sounded so sordid and intimate. I recalled that afternoon when I had walked in on Surya and my grandmother, and how excited Surya had been afterwards. What had she said that had led him to this conclusion? My grandmother was discreet and gracious. How could she ever articulate something that didn't even have a word in our language?

'Fuck, fuck, fuck!' I screamed into my pillow. We had been so bloody naive, assuming they wanted to share our lives when all they wanted to do was to take our stories and twist them out of shape. When I woke up, it was dusk, just the kind of light in which Mrs K lurked by her gate, waiting to talk to someone and share her husband's whisky. I could taste the vomit coating my tongue. I turned over, peeling my face off from the dampness of perspiration and tears and saliva that had soaked into the sheet. I returned to the book.

It concluded with a paragraph written by Surya. In

it he said that during their stay in the village, a passing conversation with a child led to the project being viewed as a treasure hunt. 'The boy asked me why I was there and I spontaneously responded that we were looking for treasure.'

I had thought of myself as Surya's companion and confidant, not some random child. I was offended but my rage was exhausted. I read on. 'A treasure hunt! It was a perfect analogy. We were digging, digging deep for treasure that would enable us to examine our roots.'

I washed my face, brushed my teeth and slipped out of the house to visit Mrs K. There was no mention of her in the book. I took the long route via what was left of the lake, past the glass structure that was being constructed where the village square had been. I hoped on the one hand that Surya had remembered to send her a copy of the book, and on the other that he had forgotten to do so.

ROCKFALL

'It is very steep climb, madam,' Joseph Raju warned Marcia as they prepared to set out. 'We must be careful, rocks are slippery.' But he was not worried. Foreign ladies like Marcia didn't fall. It seemed that they could do anything. They travelled alone from one country to the next. They trekked high and low without fear. They didn't send for the washing woman to have their clothes washed, they washed clothes themselves. They always smelled fresh and soapy. And they climbed rocks. All the same he cautioned Marcia, 'We must be careful, madam.' She didn't seem to hear him. She was busy writing in a small black-bound notebook.

Marcia was always jotting something down. Even when they paused briefly in their walk across the hot, arid riverbed strewn with boulders, she bent over the page, her rough, dry hair blowing across her face. Joseph, standing discreetly to the side, was looking down at the ground, but he saw the shadow of her hand as she tucked the errant strands carelessly behind her ear.

The sight catapulted him into the past. The first time he had touched his Jeeva's hair, it had been to tuck it behind her ear. They were in the church quadrangle, and a sudden gust of wind had whipped Jeeva's white dupatta about like a mainsail in the crosswind. Her cotton kurta clung to her body. Joseph had stood still, captivated.

Then the dupatta set sail, like the boats in his native town departing for the open seas. Jeeva giggled and Joseph ran after the piece of cotton. By the time he brought it back, Jeeva's hair was like a cyclone around her head, a heavy, black, silk cyclone, alive and seductive. Unable to resist, Joseph caught a strand of that piece of her and tucked it behind her ear. All this time later, he could still feel its weight on his fingers, a thick, silken, fluid weight. Jeeva giggled once more and stepped back, her eyes brilliant with excitement at his boldness.

'Come, come, Joseph, we must forge on. Got to get to the cave and down before dark,' Marcia declared.

'Yes, madam, finished writing, madam?' he enquired as he hurried up to her, his cloth shoulder bag swinging.

'Thank you, Joseph. Notes for a novel. I think I'll put you in it.'

He was to be a character in a novel? Would it be one that had a thick paper cover, with a man touching his mouth to a foreign woman's under a blue sky, with brightly coloured flowers in the background? Or maybe it would have a shadow picture pressed into shiny paper, a curvy lady holding a gun and leaning against a man in a hat. Marcia was not really curvy, more square and hard and tight. Joseph didn't know how to respond. He stared at Marcia and she stared back. Finally, he said, 'Thank you, madam,' and she laughed, hefting her backpack on her shoulders. Beads of sweat stood out on her fair skin that was turning red in the sun. She didn't seem to notice as she strode purposefully ahead, her short, sturdy legs choppy and confident.

They walked for two hours along the dry riverbed towards the dam. Washed by river water for an eternity, the rocks shone dark and intense, as if layer upon layer below the surface threw the sun's brilliance back. It was hot and hypnotic. Joseph, who had been here many times, was always impressed by the beauty of the granite. Shining, like Jeeva's hair, like her eyes.

'I am a tourist guide. Specialization – Vijayanagar Empire,' he'd told Jeeva soon after he met her in her native southern city where he was studying. She had giggled and her sister and friends who stood around her giggled like a chorus responding. The carved granite ruins of a forgotten empire seemed remote in their grimy urban reality. 'I will show you. It is beautiful,' he'd said to Jeeva.

From the moment he had first seen the blazing hot landscape of giant boulders, he had been compelled. He immediately put in a request to transfer to the region. The other tourist guides were locals. They had grown up in the granite. They took the rocks for granted, as they did the sculptural extravagance of the kingdom that had flourished there three or more centuries ago. They spent their energy wheeling and dealing, seducing young travellers who, mellowed by heat, camaraderie and cannabis, were ripe for exploration.

However golden, the tourists never interested Joseph in that way. He found them distasteful and unclean. And once he had met her, for him there was only Jeeva.

The day Jeeva had arrived among the rocks as Joseph's bride, it was 45°C. 'This is it, your famous place?' she said, looking around as they stepped down into the dusty bus stand. He nodded and had just begun to point out various features when she interrupted him to say, 'I'm so thirsty. Get me a Gold Spot, Joseph.' They only had Mangola at the shop – warm Mangola. Squeezed into the rickshaw on the way to the room he rented on the main street, Joseph tried to put his arm around Jeeva but she shrugged him away.

Jeeva was afraid to step out alone. Mosquitoes swarmed and it was rumoured that there were leopards on the outskirts of town. When she eventually ventured to the riverbed, the young men didn't look at her but made crude, leering love to scruffy sunburnt girls from foreign countries with tattered clothes and easy morals.

'My friend Kumar, also a guide, his sister is ready to befriend you,' Joseph said when Jeeva complained of boredom. 'She is training to be ladies' tailor.' But Jeeva didn't want to make friends with some local woman with a vocation.

After a few days she asked, 'Where is the movie theatre? The new Rajinikanth film must be out.'

The theatre was in the district centre, a two-hour bus ride away. They were late, but despite that, Jeeva was happy, chattering excitedly through the film. By the end, Joseph was exhausted by the imagery and the noise and the coarseness of it.

The cinema became a fortnightly event. One that Joseph dreaded. 'Three more days before movie day,' Jeeva would declare happily.

Joseph's ardour felt like the river that, dammed upstream, had transformed from a wild, gushing flow to a sludgy, polluted trickle.

Often they would meet some of the young men from town on the journey. Soon Joseph stopped going to the cinema, letting Jeeva go off with the busload that departed when the new movie came out. He renewed his passion for the rocks, taking intrepid tourists to remote meditation caves far above the riverbeds, accessible only when the waters were low.

One such intrepid tourist, Marcia, lodged in a guesthouse at the bazaar. She was exacting and had rejected many guides before she met Joseph. He thought she found him acceptable because he was quiet and left her alone when she was writing.

Marcia liked to talk to him as they walked – about her travels and her life. And she listened to him as well. When her face lit up with interest, he forgot that he didn't like her thick body and pale hair. He felt tempted to touch her strong, muscled shape. He told her about the extraordinary hidden carvings of the goddess.

'Take me to that sculpture you were telling me about, Joseph,' Marcia said after they had walked for two hours. 'The Adi shek aara Naara devi … Oh, you know I can't say it right! Will you take me?'

He had tried to take Jeeva there once. It had been difficult to persuade her to come. It had been difficult to keep going. 'I'm slipping, I'm slipping. Why do you bring me here,' she complained as he helped her. A few steps later she said, 'Oh, it's so hot. I can't go further.'

'Come, Jeeva, it is beautiful,' he had pleaded.

'Enough beauty, Joseph, it's enough, I don't want to see another stupid rock.' He walked on quietly and Jeeva muttered but followed behind.

Suddenly she'd shrieked, 'Look, look,' and pointed with her finger. Joseph, who was considerably higher by then, thought she'd seen a snake. He took out his precious binoculars, a gift from a grateful client, and tried to scan the rocks as he clambered down. The binoculars slipped and landed in a crevice.

Jeeva was standing with a rapt expression on her face.

'What happened, Jeeva?' he asked, terrified.

'Can't you see?' She pointed emphatically.

He shook his head, confused.

'That's the place. That's the exact place they shot Rajinikanth in his last hit.' She indicated the flat rock on the other side. 'The exact spot. Song sequence.' She hummed a filmy tune. 'I have to tell Somnath.'

Somnath was Jeeva's latest beau. He had a motorbike. She didn't have to weather the crowds on the bus any more. The movie events seemed to happen with greater and greater frequency. Often when Joseph returned home, Somnath was just departing, a pleased smile on his face. Joseph tried not to care.

∽

Marcia was telling Joseph about her recent break-up. 'He never saw the beauty I saw in nature,' she said of her partner.

Joseph nodded. 'Yes, yes, I am understanding. Always the exact same problem with Jeeva.'

Marcia continued, 'Once I was so mad I felt like pushing him off a cliff.'

'I have same feeling, madam. In my case, not cliff

but rocks. I am pushing off the rocks.' He turned and pointed. 'This is the place.'

'What am I looking for, Joseph? I don't see anything, no carvings.' Marcia stepped ahead carefully and peered at the rock faces.

'No, no! No carvings, Jeeva's resting place,' he said. 'There.' He pointed again. 'There is Rajinikanth song sequence rock.'

Marcia looked up, startled. 'You mean …' she said.

Joseph nodded. 'Here.' He indicated where Marcia was standing. 'Here, I pushed her off the rocks.'

'Literally? It's true?'

'Yes, madam, I am never lying. When recounting mythology I am always telling clearly that it is mythological story, not fact. When describing archaeology detail I am putting in full context, not presenting story like truth. That's why I am getting such good evaluation in my tourist guide course.' Marcia stared at him. He nodded. 'Yes, madam, 97 per cent, first rank. Same way I am always telling the truth about my life.'

Marcia scrambled backwards awkwardly. Joseph thought she was trying to imitate Jeeva. He laughed politely although he didn't think it was funny. It was no joking matter. This was a sacred spot; he had consecrated his emotion to the eternal, burning stillness of the rocks here.

He regretted showing Marcia this place. He

regretted telling her about Jeeva. He thought Marcia understood, but now her eyes were not shining but afraid, staring at him as though he were a strange, ugly animal. He felt a surge of anger as he stepped towards her, and thrust his arms forward with a snarl. Marcia staggered and fell.

After a moment's silence, Joseph's sense of correctness, of formality, reasserted itself. He advised Marcia to be careful, just as he had advised Jeeva. Jeeva had answered, alternately begging and screeching, her voice echoing and distorted. He had covered his ears and left.

Marcia didn't respond at all. If she was going to play games, he would leave her. 'I am returning to the town now, madam,' he bent down and called into the crevice. His voice echoed back faintly: madam, madam, mad …

PREVIOUSLY PUBLISHED

'Polymorphism' was published in *Eclectica Magazine*, April/May 2014, and was chosen to appear in their 2016 20th Anniversary Speculative Fiction Anthology.

'Intensive Care' appeared in *Nether Fortnight* 1, October/November 2010, and subsequently in the *Nether* print edition, December 2010.

'Adoration' appeared in *Pangea, an Anthology of Stories from Around the Globe*, edited by Indira Chandrasekhar and Rebecca Lloyd, Thames River Press, 2012.

'Should I Weep' appeared in *Eclectica Magazine*, April/May 2010, and was shortlisted in the *Mslexia* New Writing Competition 'Into the Deep' in July 2010.

'The Embryotic' appeared in *Cosmonauts Avenue* in March 2015. A version of the story, entitled 'The Boil', was shortlisted in the *Mslexia* Short Story Competition, 2012.

'She Can Sing' appeared in *Far Enough East* in July 2013.

'My Kitchen, My Space' appeared in *r.kv.r.y*, July 2012.

A version of 'Abandoned Rooms' was published in *Emprise Review* in September 2011, and was chosen for reprinting in the October 2012 issue of *Necessary Fiction*.

'Lennard-Jones Potentials' appeared in *Out of Print*, December 2011.

'We Read the News' appeared in *Kitaab's Writers Connect* in December 2009 and in *The Little Magazine*, January 2010.

A version of 'The Perfect Shot' appeared in *Pratilipi*, Winter 2011. The story was inspired by a lecture by Ram Rahman on Indian photographers from the 1940s through the Nehruvian era to the 1970s, given at Jnanapravaha, Mumbai, in 2010.

'The Shift' appeared in *Loquacious Placemat*, March 2010.

'Does the Word Even Exist in Our Language?' appeared in *Guftugu*, July 2016.

'Rockfall' appeared in *Pangea, an Anthology of Stories from Around the Globe*, edited by Indira Chandrasekhar and Rebecca Lloyd, Thames River Press, 2012.

ACKNOWLEDGEMENTS

My faith in myself as a writer is due to James. Selective yet voracious in his own reading, in reviewing my work, he focused through the distractions of uncertain words and unwieldy phrasing to reach the core of each story.

It makes me smile to imagine my father looking through this collection. I suspect he would find it dwells too much on the internal, but I know he would be proud. It is to my mother – with her quiet nonconformism that manifests even while respecting social norms, whose extraordinary daily courage, and whose love of the short story play no small part in inspiring my writing – to whom I dedicate this work.

My grandmother, Sooka, my mother and many wonderful aunts filled our lives with stories from family, community and mythology. Those threads of heroism, tragedy, love and the ridiculous have mutated and evolved and been woven into my works. I acknowledge this legacy with regard and gratitude.

I thank Mary Brunner for her caring reading and her pleasure in my development as a writer. Samhita Arni's warm inclusivity introduced me to a wide literary milieu. Mira and Jai with their clear, clean input have kept my writing honest, moving me away from poetic excesses.

Three online groups – Write Words, Zoetrope and Caferati – opened up worlds of literature and publishing. Through the first, I met exquisite writer, friend and mentor, Rebecca Lloyd.

To Elizabeth and Richard Meryman and the havens of creative inspiration they nurture, I am grateful. I only wish I could have shared the publication with Dick.

Dumbie evokes the magic in her work when she talks about it. I thank her for the use of her images, and bow to Rob Singleton's skills and calm generosity in creating the cover, especially when a family emergency of somewhat monumental proportions threw everything askew.

I could not have immersed myself in the writing without the help of Silpina and Mary. A debt of gratitude for their kind and unstinting support, as also to Rama and Harish and, in the past, to Leena, Jean, Joachim and Joseph.

I am proud that Karthika and Ajitha G.S., who believed in this collection, both champions of literary fiction, signed on the book.

My gratitude to editor Prema Govindan and to Bonita Shimray and her design team.

Last, but not the least, I must say thank you to Ajit. I feel lucky to have someone who supports me in all my ventures with the kindness and enthusiasm he does.